# ISOLDE'S DREAM
## and Other Stories

## SUDHIR JAIN

BAYEUX

Bayeux Arts Inc.
Isolde's Dream and other stories
Sudhir Jain

© 2007 Sudhir Jain
Published by:
Bayeux Arts Incorporated
119 Stratton Crescent S.W.
Calgary, Alberta, Canada  T3H 1T7

Printed and bound in Canada

**Library and Archives Canada Cataloguing in Publication**

Jain, Sudhir, 1938-
    Isolde's dream : and other stories / Sudhir Jain.

ISBN 978-1-896209-91-3

I. Title.

PS8619.A37I86 2007        C813'.6        C2007-901483-6

First Published: April 2007

The publisher gratefully acknowledges the assistance of the
Alberta Foundation for the Arts, the Canada Council for the Arts,
and the Government of Canada through the Book Publishing
Industry Development Program.

Cover Image: The Spring (Le Printemps), Marc Chagall (1887-
1985/Russian), Oil on Canvas. Reprinted with pemission.

# ISOLDE'S DREAM
## and Other Stories

Acknowledgement

The poem "Song of the Wayfarer" is from a booklet accompanying the CD /Mahler: Lieder Eines Fahrenden Gessellen etc,/ Thomas Hampson, Wiener Philharmoniker, Leonard Bernstein, Deutche Grammophon. Translation, Lionel Salter.

The poem "Dream" is from /Wagner and His Isolde/ by Gustav Kobbe, (New York:Dodd, Mead and Company, 1905).

Best efforts were made to obtain permission for use of the above.

To Kahlo and Asha for getting me started
and Evelyn for keeping me going.

# Contents

The Song of a Wayfarer     9

A Traveler's Diary     31

Joys of a Doctor's Husband     65

My Writing Career     79

Friends, Really!     113

Two Sides of a Coin     141

Cabbie     151

Lost and Found on a Mountain     157

Two Letters     167

A Memorable Journey     173

Isolde's Dream     181

# The Song of a Wayfarer

## 1

*At long last the sky stopped thundering and fireworks stopped. There had not been an enemy bomber in the air for several minutes. Men, women and children came out from their hiding places and looked at the smoldering ruins their homes had become. Very young children, not yet encumbered with the worries of daily living, got together to play the games of hide and seek or just ran around the rubble. Other children and the able-bodied men and women were inspecting the damage and trying to recover what they could. Older people were sitting on whatever they could find, too weak to do anything useful and too shocked to cry. Along with most of Germany, the city of Dresden was in ruins although no individual knew, or cared to know, the total extent of the damage.*

*There was one exception to the passive response of the older generation. A very frail old woman, with a shriveled physique and a bent back, was whimpering while searching in the shell of her home. No one knew what she was looking for, no one cared either. They had their own priorities. Every one had lost most of what they had and saving whatever they could of their own possessions came before any generous gestures. Suddenly, there was uproar. The shaky damaged roof of the house the old woman was searching came crashing down and trapped the woman who was now clutching a stack of papers.*

*Frau Marion von Weber was dead. The papers in her hands were the*

9

charred score of the Nordic Symphony by her old flame, Gustav Mahler. Much of the work of young Mahler died with the old lady.

This is the story of a time in the life of Frau von Weber; the time of hope, heartbreak and love.

## 2

It was January 1, 1880, the first day of the new decade. A fine sunny day ended a long cold spell in Leipzig and going out in the evening was possible again. Momma and I were now pleased that we had tickets for the opera. I helped her prepare a dinner of sauerkraut and Polish sausages. After dinner, I changed into a blue dress which hinted at the cleavage rather than obscenely displayed it, as was the fashion among some young unmarried women. Not that I was that young. I was hitting twenty five and the fear I would end up on the shelf was starting to cross some minds. I put on a light make up to enhance my eye lashes and thin lips and play down the nose and the chin. Precisely thirty minutes before the curtain time, a carriage took us to the Municipal Theatre. We went straight to our usual seats and flipped through the program till the conductor raised his baton. It was a captivating performance with wonderful fairyland sets and some great singing by the tenor. *Oberon* was my favourite opera; Carl Maria von Weber's last and best. What a shame the composer died so young; while visiting England to conduct this very opera. I was a tiny tot when Papa told me of the reburial ceremony of the remains of the founder of German romantic opera organized by my other favourite composer, Richard Wagner.

We were sipping coffee and watching the crowd from our vantage position in a corner in the intermission after the first act. Momma spotted Frau Wenzel, a friend she hadn't seen for a year or more and called out to her. The short round lady came over with a tall slim young army officer following close behind.

She introduced Capt. Carl von Weber to us as the grandson of the composer. Some of the lustre of the grandfather must have transferred on the modest officer. I was charmed by his courteous manner and persuaded Momma to accept when he invited us to join his group to a beer hall after the opera. Carl wanted to know all about my interests and told amusing stories about his job and the confusion his name created among opera lovers. He charmed Momma as well by his close attention to her glass. She invited him to visit us at home at his convenience.

It did not take long for Carl to ask for my hand in marriage. I accepted after due maidenly hesitation and we were married within three months of our first meeting at the fairyland opera. We moved into a comfortable home on a quiet street and settled into the life of an army officer of adequate means. Three children arrived in four years and life became hectic; yes, hectic but monotonous. Carl's charm faded as the months rolled by. We were rarely intimate and our life was a dull routine. Our only activity together was the opera. We indulged fully in the craze of the day – Wagner. Leipzig's native son was the rage, his operas as well as his books. I kept up my interest in literature by reading and my own writing. I was flattered that Carl paid due attention to my opinions on cultural issues but it did not make up for the distress caused by his full control on every thing else including the family purse.

I remember very well that fateful day; the first Friday in September 1886. There was certain excitement in the air. The whole city was excited. Gustav Mahler, a young conductor who had just joined the opera company at the Municipal Theatre was to conduct the new sumptuous production of Wagner's *Lohengrin* with a stellar cast. Carl had pulled strings to get the tickets. Anybody who considered himself somebody was going to be there. It had been widely rumoured that the king and the queen of Saxony would grace the occasion along with the widow of the composer.

*Lohengrin* was the most performed opera in Europe and the audience could never get enough of it. It was composed when Herr Wagner was living in Dresden. Its performance was not permitted in Saxony for almost a decade due to the composer's disloyalty to the king. However, all was forgiven in due course and there is not a day now without a Wagner opera in one of the theatres in Leipzig or Dresden.

The maid helped me in a tight green velvet dress with a meter long train. I applied the make up carefully and the maid brushed my long lustrous platinum hair. I put on my white silk stockings and gold embroidered shoes imported from India to enhance my appearance as I stepped forward. Carl put on his officer's uniform. When he took my arms in his to lead me to the carriage I felt a momentary rush of old feelings, "Oh, he looks as handsome now as he did the first time I saw him." As if divining my thoughts, Carl looked at me and whispered softly, "You are looking more beautiful than ever. I can only hope that some prince will not take note of you." Poor Carl! He couldn't have known how prophetic he was, even though it was not a prince who took note.

3

We arrived at the theatre early and found a good spot to observe the high society. I commented to Carl on beautiful dresses working in my mind how much they must have cost. Carl ogled at cleavages and bowed to anyone who even glanced at him. Then the five toots on a trumpet announced that the opera would begin in five minutes. We found our seat and sharply at eight, the orchestra stopped tuning and a short frail boyish figure with dark long unruly hair and prominent Jewish features darted out to the podium, bowed to the audience, turned to face the orchestra and raised his baton.

Every one in the hall was familiar with the prelude to *Lohengrin*. Not only had they seen the opera numerous times before, the prelude was a popular first piece in the concert halls. But this time it sounded more intense than ever before. The muted violins were more muted and barely audible. The sound developed in minute increments into a melancholic melody full of foreboding. After the ears and minds had adjusted to the melody, it suddenly exploded into a great crescendo and very quickly almost died down as if the accumulating tension had burst open and then calm had returned. The music then settled into its melancholic rhythm – the world was sharing the grief of a sobbing woman about to be deserted by her lover. I am sure I was not the only woman wiping tears when the curtain went up on a breathtaking scene on the bank of a river.

The whole opera was fascinating with wonderful scenery, fine singing and beautiful music played perfectly by a great orchestra under a masterful conductor. At the end, when Lohengrin pulled Duke Gottfried out of the water and boarded the boat as Elsa fell down dead, the audience took a while to recover. Then every one got up to their feet in unison and cheered till they were hoarse. The cast, the orchestra and the conductor exhausted after four hours of painstaking work, were rejuvenated by this adulation. At last the curtain came down for good and the audience started drifting out of the hall. Carl asked me on the way out whether I wanted to go and thank the conductor as was our custom when the performance was particularly good. I readily agreed.

Backstage, the prominent citizens of Leipzig and the orchestra members were jostling to shake hands with the small thin man with a broad forehead and a broader smile. If truth were known, he must have been relieved that his introduction to this city of Bach, Weber, Mendelssohn, Schumann and Wagner had gone so well. He was thanking every one for their kindness. We were the last ones to reach him. Carl introduced himself as the grandson of the celebrated composer and me as a great devotee of Wagner.

I thanked him for giving me a deeper insight into the opera and hoped he would stage an equally exciting version of *Tristan and Isolde*. Then out of the blue, Carl invited him for dinner on an evening convenient to him. Herr Mahler agreed after some hesitation and promised to send a note with suitable dates.


4


Herr Mahler arrived sharply at the appointed hour of six the following Tuesday. He told us he lived a couple of kilometers away near the opera house and had walked over. He was the only guest because he had insisted that no one else be invited. He had warned us that he was a teetotaler and had simple tastes in food. Carl greeted him and I introduced him to our three children aged two to four. He was obviously very fond of children and talked gently with them till the nurse dragged them away.

Our guest was very well read and had a wonderful way of expressing complex ideas in simple words. We discussed Wagner's essay on conducting, the philosophies of Schopenhauer and Nietzsche and the training of artists who could act as well as sing the demanding passages. After dinner, the conversation turned to the direction music had to take after Wagner. It transpired that Herr Mahler was a composer too. He had written the incidental music for a play which was touring Germany and had composed two song cycles and a small symphony and was working on a large scale work which he claimed would be grander than any purely orchestral work in repertory. He told us that he cursed the Vienna Conservatory at least once every day for not giving him the Beethoven composition prize and thus consigning him to the brutal life of a conductor rather than the noble and contented one of a composer. We were both touched and I got him to promise that he would play his music for us next time he visited us.

After Herr Mahler had left, Carl wondered aloud if he was the right man to complete the opera from the sketches his grandfather had left and the two succeeding generations had carefully preserved. I reminded him that the great composers like Schumann and Meyerbeer had declined the opportunity because of inherent difficulties and it may not be an undertaking for a young composer. In any case, we did not know how good Herr Mahler was as a composer. Carl agreed and we decided to look into his credentials as a composer before raising the issue.

None of our musical friends had heard of any composition by our new conductor. When a friend of Carl asked the impresario of the Municipal theatre, Herr Staegmann, he replied that if he knew of such ambitions in his new conductor, the 'boy' would still be unemployed in Prague. Thus, when Herr Mahler arrived with a rather slim folder under his arm one Sunday afternoon, we had given up on him as the saviour of the fading notes in Carl's possession.

After a tall glass of water Herr Mahler inquired about the children. I asked the nurse to bring them in. He presented them with little toys suitable for their ages and chatted with each of them. After the children were taken away, he opened the folder. I noticed the title *Songs of the Wayfarer* on the folder. "I wrote the poems and set them to music a couple of years ago and they can be sung by a soprano or a baritone," he told us as he gave the music of alternate songs to me and Carl. He advised us to carefully look at the words when he knocked about on the piano to get its feel. "Singer must convey the feeling, the rest follows naturally," he said adjusting the piano stool for his rather short stature.

We could see from his "knocking about" that he was a wonderful pianist. When Carl complimented him on his playing, his reply surprised us by its audacity, "I was enrolled at the Conservatory as a piano student till I heard Liszt play. That concert convinced me that I was never going to be that good and

I switched to Composition. I conduct to make a living and live to compose."

After a brief look at the score, Carl asked to be excused from singing because the songs were too difficult for him, he could not express the deep melancholy in them. I took over the sheaf from him and spent a few minutes studying the music. "Ready?" he asked when I looked up. I nodded agreement and he started playing the first song about the beloved marrying someone else. I did my best to convey the disappointment and grief in the poem and he seemed quite pleased. "Better than some professional singers," I remember him having said. The same routine followed with all four songs, each more sad than the one before. I was emotionally exhausted as I sang the last lines:

> Under the linden tree
> Which snowed its blossoms on me,
> I knew not of life's pain,
> All, all was well again-
> All, all,
> Love and grief,
> My world, my dreams.

Carl was deeply touched, "The words and the music come from a broken heart. I hope you will find a new love to mend your heart, my friend." I was deeply moved by the grief in those sheets. I secretly pledged to help the poor man recover from his sorrowful state and protect him from falling in it again. I suggested that with proper orchestration the songs would have the power to melt the heart of a glacier and expressed the hope that we would be able to hear them with full orchestra and the professional singers. He was not very optimistic, "With the workload at the opera, and the tone poem I am working on, there is little time to promote my music for now." Then a glorious smile lit his face, "The tone poem will be a great work that will open all doors. I better wait for that." Carl jumped at the idea of a tone poem, "Well, what a wonderful idea, a tone poem. Something like Liszt used to compose. I do hope we will get to hear it as it progresses."

We did not hear anything from Herr Mahler for a couple of weeks. I was surprised to note how much I was missing him. His unruly hair, infectious laugh, even the strange walk, but most of all his intellectual approach to everything was carving a space in my heart. I wondered whether I liked him because in every way I could think of, he was the opposite of Carl. Even the kids were asking when he would visit next. I resisted the temptation of inviting him over, if only to keep Carl from suspecting my growing attachment.

One night when we had just gone to sleep we heard loud knocks on the door. Carl went to see who was disturbing our sleep while I watched through a crack in the door. It was a very excited Herr Mahler with a sheaf of papers in his hands. "I have just completed the first movement of my tone poem. You said you will like to hear it when it is done. I am here to play it for you." He rushed past Carl to the piano. I threw a dress on and joined them. Carl and I stood behind him looking at the score as he played it. The sound was new and unfamiliar, but very pleasant to the ear. It was a long piece, almost twenty minutes. He made descriptive comments as he played, indicating the instruments in the orchestra which would be playing. We stood there mesmerized, not a yawn between us. After playing the last note, he sat still for a while, then put the piano lid down, turned around and looked at our beaming faces, "I thank you from the bottom of my heart for bearing with me at this late hour. I just had to share the ecstasy of creation with someone."

"We thank you for making us the first listeners of what promises to be a great work," we both replied in unison. He declined the offer of a drink, collected the music and staggered home exhausted but happy.

Next morning Carl asked me whether I had changed my mind about showing Herr Mahler the sketches of his grandfather's opera. The thought of having a great excuse to be with the young man appealed to me as much as having the opera finished. I agreed, hopefully not too heartily. Carl sent him a note suggesting a meeting to discuss an issue of artistic importance without stating what it was. He invited us to meet him in his office at the opera house in between the rehearsals the next day.

Carl collected the box of carefully preserved papers and we took a carriage to the Municipal theatre. He greeted us with his charming smile and led us to a small office just large enough to fit a desk, three chairs and a filing cabinet. "This is where I study the music before the rehearsals and meet with the artists," he told us. Carl thanked him for sparing his time, pulled out the papers and said, "After the untimely death of my grandfather, the sketches of a comic opera, *Die Drei Pintos*, were found among his papers. My father and I have preserved these for sixty years. Will you like to look at these and consider completing it? I have written a libretto from his notes to make things easy for the composer. We can help you with any revisions in the libretto but first you have to decide whether it is worth your while. Our only wish is that the completed work has the feel of a Weber work of the twenties rather than that of a modern work. We do not expect any financial returns. All royalties will go to you if you agree to take on the task." I nodded in agreement. Herr Mahler took the papers and thumbed through them. "Well, it is certainly worth a look. I will give it a priority and determine if I can do a creditable job. If I can do it, then I will decide how best to proceed. I will see you both here at the same time next week." He stood up and thanked us for trusting him with the family heirloom. He was thoughtful as he saw us off in the lobby. I hoped that Herr Mahler felt the same way as I did about this assignment.

He seemed quite excited on our next visit. When Carl called him Herr Mahler he almost exploded, "No, No, I am Gustav. And if you don't consider it impertinent, you are Carl and the lady I have come to admire so much is Marion." When we got to the office, he closed the door before continuing, "Let us keep it quiet. I will take on the challenge. There are some great things going for it. Your grandfather is justifiably very popular in Saxony and even the performances of *Euryanthe* are sold out. A long lost opera by this great man is sure to be popular if it is presented properly. The story is very funny. Audiences love masquerade and three lovers chasing one woman gives us many opportunities for funny scenes. The libretto is good but it can be improved here and there. The music needs to be arranged with care. It will take a few months to complete the whole thing and it will be my pleasure to work with you. Once the poems are finished, music will not take long. I am looking into other Weber works for the clues on harmony and the melody lines and there is very little that would need to be new."

Carl seemed relieved to hear this, "This is the best news I have had for a long time. My late father and grandfather will be so happy and surely bless us all from their abode in heaven."

"I can meet with you on Tuesday and Thursday afternoons to work on it and play the music as it progresses. The tone poem can wait; it is going to be put aside for now."

"Gustav, I am sorry I have to be away on most afternoons. I am sure Marion can work with you without the idle tongues of Leipzig wagging. Can't you sweetheart?"

My heart took a leap at the prospect of spending afternoons together by ourselves, "Of course, dear."

Four thousand minutes to Tuesday afternoon passed slowly. Gustav knocked on the door a few minutes after two. After a polite exchange of greetings, he took out three sheets of paper and gave them to me, "Songs the kids might like to sing, one for each." I was thrilled. It was the first time in two generations that any music had been composed specifically for the family. He played with the children for a short while before I asked the nurse to take them for their nap. When we were alone he took my hands in his, looked in my eyes and said, "It is for you alone I am doing this. To spend a while with you for any reason whatsoever will make my days worthwhile."

"Gustav, you are being silly. We are both being silly because I liked what you said. I was praying you would agree so I could be with you. We have to stop this stupidity though. Falling in love won't do. I am a married woman with three little children."

"Yes, three lovely children. It may be too late for me though."

"You are being silly again. Let us do what you are here for." Gustav sighed, sat down on a straight back chair, resumed his intellectual air and outlined the story he thought the illustrious composer had in mind and what improvements could be made in Carl's libretto. "Carl has done a good job. We need a bigger role for Innkeeper's daughter Inez to balance male voices in the first act. Don Gomez should be less of a comic character, Gaston scheming but not evil and Don Pinto more gauche. It was clever of Carl to give prominent roles to Gaston's valet and Clarissa's maid Laura."

"Clarissa should be funny, but stronger and her father Pantaleone a little more dignified," I put in.

"Yes, yes, indeed. It will make more sense then," he agreed. He pulled out a red pencil, sang the words, stopped to think and made changes, sometimes rewriting the whole passage "to suit the music I have in mind." He asked me to read Inez, Laura and Clarissa's passages. He carefully listened to my suggestions and often followed them, particularly when they related to Clarissa. He handed me the sheet as he finished the "edited version" and I made a neat copy.

I waited for our afternoons with mixed emotions. I wanted him to express the feelings I knew he had rather than bottle them up.

But I also knew that I would be embarrassed if he did and wouldn't know how to control my emotions. He took me at my word and was very proper for the three weeks it took to complete the revision.

We finished a little earlier that Thursday. It was a beautiful autumn afternoon and the nurse had taken the children out to play in the park. He put the pencil down, looked straight into my soul, mumbled something unintelligible, cleared his throat, went behind my chair, put his arms around me and whispered in my right ear, "You are the light of my life; you are the reason for living." I could feel his hot breath on my cheek and I turned my moistened eyes towards him. His full lips met mine and I pulled his face closer still. The tears mingled on our faces as we expressed our love with silent words full of meaning.

6

Carl was quite pleased with the changes and Gustav set about arranging the music. His workload at the Municipal theatre had become very heavy due to the sickness of maestro Nikisch, the music director of the company. Hence, the progress was slow and it was the following October when the work was complete. It would have taken longer if Gustav were not so methodical. First, he completed seven scenes that grandpa had left extensive notes on. Then he picked the music from his relatively unknown operas and other compositions and modified it to suit many of the remaining scenes. Finally, he wrote an interlude and the finale based on themes from the selected numbers and re-scored the whole piece for uniformity.

Poor Gustav, he tried so hard to be Weber of 1820 but the Mahler of 1887 could not be altogether suppressed. Still, the whole opera made sense. To iron out the wrinkles, we planned a private performance of the completed work one Sunday evening after the children were in bed and the nurse had gone home, with half of the composing duo on our piano and, hopefully, the other half watching over it in spirit.

Late on the following Thursday, Carl received an order from his regiment to be in Dresden. There was no way he could get out of it. He told me to go ahead with the 'premiere' as he called it. Gustav was surprised to find me alone when he arrived but he said he was impatient to hear the whole work played out and see what changes were needed. There was a space in the schedule at the theatre next January due to an unforeseen cancellation. He wanted to show it to Herr Staegmann to persuade him to stage it in that space. After a drink of grape juice, Gustav settled on the piano and I sat down next to him to turn the page. He played with gusto, just as the comedy required and sang all parts as his idol Wagner used to do. Only, Gustav was an excellent pianist unlike the Master but his singing barely made the passing grade. In short breaks between the acts he loved my apfel strudel but I stuck to fruit. However, he was focused on music and did not profess his love for me even once. By now, I had come to know him well enough not to be surprised or offended.

He finished with great relish, singing in full voice the final song when Gaston, his valet, and the chorus get together with Clarissa and her father to celebrate love and life. Thankfully it did not wake up the children. He got up laughing uproariously and I clapping heartily. He put his arms around my waist, picked me up and gave me a whirl. Then he lost control and we fell on the sofa, I on top of him. We lay there recovering our breath. After a short while he tried to speak but I stopped him by putting my mouth firmly over his. It wasn't long before I felt he was ready and we made love for the first time. As if in a dream, he kept repeating, "You have given a new meaning to my life." It was heavenly.

Gustav came in out of breath on the following Friday afternoon. He told us excitedly without even greeting us, "Herr Staegmann loved the opera. He wants a production worthy of the company. He has invited the King, nobility and all the great names in 'music industry' of Germany for the premiere on January 20. I have only three months to prepare. Still, this is an opportunity to establish my credentials as a composer. On the other hand, anything but a great show would be bad for Leipzig and end my career." He rushed out and left Carl and me thinking how child-like a great artist can be. I wondered if he would have left in such a hurry if Carl were away.

During the next three months we made full use of a handful of opportunities we got to be alone. I am afraid I had become less hospitable to Carl and he must have noticed that something was different. He did not say anything though, probably because he was enthralled with the preparations of the opera and did not let an opportunity pass to demonstrate how much effort he had put in to get his grandfather's sketch to this stage. He was noted on the billboards as the librettist and even strangers stopped on the street to compliment him.

At last, the long-awaited evening arrived! Carriages started arriving at the theatre an hour before the performance. From them emerged the high society of Saxony, ladies in beautiful gowns with long trains and gentlemen in uniforms bedecked with medals. The program sellers did a brisk business because every one wanted extra copies as mementoes of the occasion. Carl Maria von Weber was to Leipzig what Wolfgang Mozart was to Salzburg. A new production of any of his established operas was a big event. This being the first production of his "long lost work," it was so much more special. The air was thick with anticipation. Carl was the darling of the crowd and his autograph was much in demand. I had to pull him away to get to our seats on time. No sooner had we sat down, cheers erupted from the audience. The royal couple had taken their seats in their box and their faithful subjects were expressing their joy.

At the last minute Gustav decided to omit the overture because it did not quite match the opera and, after a very brief prelude, the opera opened in an inn with young men having fun. The audience enjoyed the playful repartees between the innkeeper's daughter Inez and the young man on the make, Gaston. Entry of the simpleton Don Pinto who is on his way to marry Clarissa, and the scene in which Gaston teaches Pinto how to court a noble woman, had the audience rolling in the aisles. The delightful chorus which ends the first act with Pinto asleep and Gaston on his way to Madrid with Pinto's letter of introduction to Pantaleone in his hands brought the audience to their feet.

A very pleasant interlude introduced a rather short second act in which Pantaleone announces the arranged marriage of his daughter Clarissa with Don Pinto and orders a celebration, while Clarissa is pledging herself to Don Gomez. The third act has a lot of action. Gaston appears in the garb of Pinto to claim Clarissa, then agrees to facilitate the marriage of the two lovers and let Gomez pretend he is Pinto. Eventually the real Pinto arrives on the scene. However, he makes a fool of himself and is thrown out, the two lovers are united and the opera ends with a short but thundering chorus.

The crowd erupted as the curtain came down. Every one in the audience stood up and clapped and cheered till they were exhausted. I lost count of the curtain calls. Gustav, who had joined the performers on stage, waved to Carl to take a bow. Carl was glowing as he made his way to the front of the hall. The curtain finally came down for good and we made our way backstage. Gustav was surrounded by the members of the orchestra, performers and stage hands, every one trying to reach him to shake his hands. He was thanking every one who extended a hand to him. The crowd thinned after a while and he spotted me looking adoringly at his face. He made his way to me, lifted me up by the waist for the people to see me clearly as if showing a trophy he had just won and said loudly, "The luminous being, entirely devoted to beauty and good, she is the person I credit with the success of this opera." Every one clapped while Carl watched perplexed. Gustav noticed this, put me down gently and raised Carl's hand, "Ladies and gentleman, the man we all have to thank for this sweet moment. Not only did he protect the legacy of a great man for sixty years, he enhanced it by his work on the poems." Now the cheers were for Carl and he was evidently pleased.

Herr Staegmann invited us to join his select group for a celebration of his creation. He was quick to claim the triumphant show as his own. Had it failed, it would have been Gustav's alone. In any event, the party was a big affair. Plenty to eat and drink and every one had a lot to say. Gustav as usual abstained from alcohol but he said again and again how good every one was in the production. After the party, he accepted our offer to take him to his home in our carriage. On the way he surprised us by saying, "I have the other four movements of the tone poem fully formed in my head. It will be down on paper in a few weeks. It will confirm my status as a leading composer and allow me to give up conducting." On this happy note he thanked us, got out of the carriage and walked to the door of his rather modest rooming house.


7


Gustav paid a surprise visit to me one late evening when Carl was in Dresden. He had brought several folders of music tied neatly in multi-coloured ribbons which he ceremoniously handed to me. "This is my humble offering to the woman I love more than I love music, or life. What you have in your hands are songs for your children, the only copies of an opera and a symphony I wrote in my student years, and *Blumine*, the second movement of my tone poem. The words of dedication do not express all my feelings for

25

you but they do not need to because you are aware of them. These are for you to keep. I hope it will give you some pleasure to own them."

I looked at his face which had become luminous with the love he felt for me. My eyes swelled with tears and the folders dropped from my hands. He led me to the settee where we sat side by side looking tearfully at each other. After a few minutes, he went to the piano and played *Blumine*. I was transported to a new world while listening to the glorious serenade. When he finished, he took my hands, bent down and kissed them. Then without a word, he left closing the door silently behind him.

By the end of March, the tone poem was finished. He played it to us on one long evening, from the remarkable spring dawn opening we had heard before to the heroic finale. It was hard to imagine how the alter ego of Grandpa Weber could invent these new sounds and integrate them with such skill. Carl shook his hands vigorously and kept repeating, "Friend, your conducting days are over; a great composer is born." I sensed that the tone poem was Gustav's expression of his love for me. I managed to control my emotions but I am certain that Gustav knew that I knew.

Carl and I saw Gustav two weeks later after he conducted a performance of *The Barber of Baghdad* by Cornelius. Although he used the new orchestration, Gustav managed to bring out the original charm of the music to the great delight of the audience. Backstage, as usual with him, Gustav was praising every one for the success. He thanked Carl for coming to see him and slipped a ball of paper in my hand when no one was looking.

I straightened the paper as soon as I was alone. I must say it was not entirely unexpected. "Dear Marion: I can't live without you. Gustav needs his Marion the way Richard needed his Cosima. Only way I can expand the world of orchestral music is with Marion by my side. To accomplish this we must leave Leipzig

26

and move somewhere distant. I am resigning from my job and leaving town next month. I have invitations from all over Germany to conduct new productions of *Die Drei Pintos*. I think we can live comfortably from the royalties. There is also a strong possibility of a job in Budapest. Will you come with me?"

How can I leave my babies? How can I be without Gustav? Can I live with the guilt if Gustav gives up composing? Is Art more important than the three lives I have brought into this world? Will Gustav's Art be enough compensation for my guilt of leaving the children with Carl without their mother? What is more important: loving a genius to nurture his creativity or mothering? The questions whirled in my mind without resolution. There was no one I could turn to for help.

A week went by. Carl must have noticed my confused state. He asked again and again if I was all right. He even suggested calling a midwife to see if I were pregnant. But I pretended I had a headache, nothing bad, just a niggling one. One evening Carl came home quite disturbed. He had heard that Gustav was leaving Leipzig. He seemed more upset about not being told than by the departure of a friend. I feigned surprise. He sent a note inviting him to drop by when he could.

Gustav showed up the next evening. He looked as if he had not slept for several days. His eyes were swollen, he face was unshaved and clothes rumpled. Carl asked, "Why are you leaving if it is causing you so much grief?"

"There are times when one has to take the bull by the horns. It is such a time for me," he answered looking sideways at me. His mournful glance reminded me of the *Wayfarer* songs I had sung a year ago and the promise to save him from further grief I had made to myself that day. The sky cleared and I knew what I had to do. I made an excuse and went to my room. I wrote a short note, "Yes, I will be your Marion. I will meet you at the station on the day you set for us to leave." I rolled it into a ball and returned to join the men in my past and the future. I passed the note to Gustav behind Carl's back.

The next day I received a note tactfully addressed to both of us informing me that the sedate hausfrau would do the unthinkable on the morning of May 17, just two weeks away. When Carl read the note aloud, the dam broke and sobbing uncontrollably I told Carl what I planned to do. Carl got up from his chair, went to the window and looking at the dark clouds gathering on the horizon said, "I am not as dumb as I may appear to be. I have long suspected that all was not above board. Frau Wenzel also warned me of the brewing scandal. I did not confront the issue because I cannot afford to lose my commission in the army. Now that things are in the open, let me say this. I will not assert my rights and force you to do your duty. You still have two weeks to change your mind. To make things easy for you, I will leave town the day before the departure. I can only hope that the sense of what is right for your dear family will prevail." He turned around, patted my shoulders as he passed me and went out.

Poor Carl! Gentleman to the fingertips.


## 8

On May 16 Carl left for Dresden dressed in his full uniform. He seemed a bit tense but no more than he had been since our confrontation. I was doing all I could to control my emotions. He kissed me before he boarded the carriage to take him to the station and said, "I trust you will do what you consider best in the circumstances." I managed to hold my tears and spent the evening trying to pack the few essentials which I would need. Then I started writing the parting note to Carl. It was proving to be even more difficult than I had expected. In his own way he had been a kind husband, had provided reasonably, was not possessive and jealous like most husbands and if he was somewhat commonplace I knew it when I married him. It would be hard for him to raise the children. But I had to follow my destiny and nurture a genius.

I must have nodded off on my writing desk. I was startled by the loud shouts at the door. I rushed to open it. Carl, unsteady on his feet, was firmly held by two policemen. Another policeman, the sergeant, was behind them carrying a gun which I knew was Carl's. Carl was mumbling something in a drunken stupor but fell silent when he saw me. I asked every one in. They sat Carl down on the straight back chair. Soon he had closed his eyes and started snoring. The sergeant told me that he had to give Carl a strong sedative to control him. Then he told me what had happened.

The railway compartment Carl boarded for Dresden was quite crowded. The heat was suffocating and the air filled with pungent tobacco smoke. As the train pulled out of the station and passengers settled down for their journey, Carl asked a man playing a guitar next to the window whether he could open it. The man refused rather curtly. Something snapped in Carl's head. He started shouting, "To hell with the Artists, to hell with the Musicians," and started shooting randomly but fortunately above the heads. The passengers cowered down and women started screaming. Two big men eventually overpowered Carl and took away his gun. He was handed over to the policemen who had brought him home.

I put Carl to bed and spent the night in a chair next to him. He slept fitfully most of the night under the influence of the drug and had an excruciating headache in the morning. The doctor heard the story, thoroughly examined him, and prescribed complete rest for a week. He took me aside, "Frau von Weber, Herr von Weber needs careful monitoring. There is nothing wrong with his body; it is the mind that is disturbed. You have to watch him every minute of the day. I wish both of you luck."

My destiny, it turned out, was to care for a sick husband for

29

the next twenty years. Gustav's destiny was to reach great heights as conductor, to marry a selfish woman who caused him immense grief and to compose heart-breaking symphonies and songs. I am sure his memories of the time we tried to find love and happiness faded. But I remember every single event vividly because I had the manuscripts of his early music to cherish and not much else to fill the vacuum. Fate was unkind to us both. Neither of us knew love again although we pretended we did. We did not know happiness either; one can pretend to love but pretending does not bring happiness.

# A Traveler's Diary

## 1

It happened when we were living in London, England. Evelyn's birthday was fast approaching and I didn't know what to do. It was too late to plan a surprise party. In any event, there is always someone who tries to curry her favour by breaking the news and ruining the surprise. Fortunately, there was still time to book a table for dinner in the world renowned restaurant where the mighty got together to settle the fate of mankind. As often happens to me, there was a rather dark cloud in the otherwise sunny sky. Her birthday fell on Friday, a popular evening for dining out. I called the restaurant from the office the moment the thought sparked ripples in my brain cells. "Sorry sir," the syrupy voice of *maitre'd* came back, "We are booked solid. We do have a few tables which we keep for hotel guests. If you were planning to stay the night, I could book you a nice table next to our flower display. Of course, sir, the hotel reception will have to confirm the room reservation."

It occurred to me that a night at Ahoy may not be a bad idea. We had been so busy with our jobs that romance was being drained out of our lives, even though we had been married only a few months. Why not make it a whole weekend, I thought. A long romantic dinner in the seductive aroma of flower display followed by a roll in the hay, as they say, and an English breakfast of fried eggs and bacon in bed with no worries about checking out. Nothing to beat it, I decided. I called the hotel reservation and booked a room over the weekend. I requested them to inform the restaurant of the reservation. I called the restaurant an hour later to make sure every thing was in order.

I told Evelyn of my plan for her birthday over the dinner of leftover shepherd's pie. She was delighted but only for a second. Then she screamed, "Oh my God, what would I wear." I suggested a couple of dresses I liked. "They won't do. It is Ahoy we are going to. Aren't we? Who knows which grandee we bump into? We need to feel as if we go there every day. I will need to get a new pant suit."

The time I am talking about was the glory days of female emancipation; early sixties of the last century. Women's fashion had taken two opposite directions at the same time, the kind of thing only possible with women's fashion. At the one end, the skinny model Twiggy had popularized mini skirts so short that older men modestly looked the other way when younger ones ogled and gave their imagination a free rein. At the other end, women started wearing pants, not only at home but at work as well. To go with the pants they wore tunics reaching the mid thighs, which miniskirts never did. For reasons beyond any man's comprehension, they still wore stockings under the pants.

Somehow Evelyn found time to go to Oxford Street and acquire a bluish green silk pant suit, a stylish handbag and a suitable scarf; scarves were then taking over from the hats. Of course, she had to get matching shoes which she was able to find in the store next door specializing in Italian fashions. She came home delighted with her purchases and instructed me to make sure that I looked like her husband, not a toy boy. In other words, I had to buy a new suit, matching shirt and a tie. The stars were in their proper places on the following day, the tailor agreed to have the suit ready on the day of the dinner.

The day arrived. We packed our suitcases, which still looked reasonable in spite of some rough handling on our honeymoon. We took a cab to Ahoy and I gave a large tip to the driver to impress the porter. He in turn expected an equally large tip for carting the cases to the reception desk, as did the porter who transported them to the room. Once in the room, we showered and dressed with care. After finishing her make up, Evelyn helped me with the tie and gold cuffs and I admired her appearance while helping with her sapphire necklace. Five minutes before our reservation time, we checked each other one more time and took the elevator to the second floor.

I led the way to the restaurant, Evelyn following a little behind. She was not quite comfortable in her new shoes and did not have the spring in her feet that I had. The *maitre'd* greeted me heartily but his countenance changed when he saw Evelyn. He looked from her toes to her face, as if judging her for some contest, than sadly nodded his head. "Sorry, sir," he uttered his favourite phrase and added, "Pant suits are not allowed in the dining room."

I was annoyed. "You are wearing a pant suit. And you are standing in the dining room."

"Sorry, sir. Women in pant suits are not allowed in the dining room. Not much I can do. Rules are rules. We all have to follow them. Where would the British Empire be without rules?"

"But British Empire has evaporated from the face of the Earth with all its rules."

"Sorry sir, Ahoy has a tradition of sticking to the rules. I am not authorized to tinker with what has stood the test of time."

Just when I was about to say something unpleasant, Evelyn put a hand on my shoulder. She pointed to the Ladies Washroom and asked me to wait for a couple of minutes. She was back in one hundred and fifteen seconds. I looked at her amazed. Pants were gone, probably neatly folded in her hand bag. What she had on was a dress with the skirt only slightly longer than a mini. The *maitre'd* glanced at her long legs precariously balanced on super high heels and looked pleased. He guided us to our table next to a gorgeous display from an English country garden.

The dinner that followed was just the beginning of a weekend to remember.

## 2

Everything seemed to be in its proper place in the Kingdom of Libya when I read *Little Black Sambo* to my two year old daughter Roshan before kissing her good night. Evelyn was preparing for a picnic she was planning for the next day with her brother Thomas who was visiting us from England. Poor Thomas! It took all of three weeks for him to recover from the bug he picked up on a tiring journey of two and a half hours on a British Airways plane from London to Tripoli followed by a vicious attack of diarrhea known to expatriates as Tripoli Trots. No one with a heart could blame him for not venturing far from the villa. Moreover, the roads in our neighbourhood had been dug up to lay down the sewerage pipes. One had to park the cars some distance away and cross the man made ditches on narrow shaky planks. Being seven month pregnant, Evelyn hadn't pushed her brother so far. But the thought of him returning home without leaving the immediate surroundings of our modest residence was too much to bear. In his last week, Evelyn decided that she had to show him a little of the Libyan coastline and its history. She planned a drive to the Roman ruins of Sabratha two hours by car. When she was organising the food and drinks for three of them, Thomas studied the map to determine the best route. After a serious examination lasting almost an hour, he concluded that the highway running along the coast was the best option. Libya's other highway ran South from Tripoli to the heart of Sahara desert and was navigable only in a Jeep.

We went to bed after wishing each other good night and pleasant dreams. I slept like a log till six and don't remember having any dreams, pleasant or otherwise. As was my custom, I got up quietly, dressed, had my breakfast of granola especially made by Evelyn from the ingredients from the souk and left for work with the rest of the family still in the slumber land.

It was a bright, warm and pleasant morning, like any other morning of the first day of September in Tripoli. The heat of summer was a bad memory and cool winter mornings were a few weeks away. I negotiated all the planks with no trouble and hopped into my trusty Fiat 600. It was a wonderful little car; well suited to skim over sand tracks we called streets. Two small skinny adults and two young children could snugly fit in it and the trunk was just big enough for a briefcase and a handbag. The 600 cc engine was big for the light as feather car and it had great acceleration. I loved it.

There was no traffic on the coast road when I got on it. This did not strike me as unusual for that hour - I always tried to reach the office before the crowd to secure one of the few shady spots in the parking lot. It wasn't long before I was at the junction of two major roads appropriately named after the heroes of the struggle for independence. Sciara Omar Mokhtar ran along the coast north of the city to the harbour and Sciara El Senussi skirted the inner city to the south. As I headed towards the harbour road, a young soldier came out of the shade of the palm tree, blocked my path and signaled me to take the other road. I took this diversion in my stride because the roads were frequently closed to the public to let the motorcade of the members of royal family pass unhindered by other traffic. For a country of a million people, Libya had a lot of claimants to this privilege.

Sciara El Senussi was a round about way to get to Mobil, my employer, but I was in no hurry. Eventually I came to the road with the King's palace on the right and restaurants and offices on the left. Mobil was housed in the last building just past a gas station and across the palace gate. A back street between the gas station and the building led to the parking lot. While passing the gas station I noticed several gun toting kids in army uniform milling around the pumps. As I turned on to the back street, a teenager barely able to carry the heavy gun on his shoulder stepped in front of the car and asked in Arabic, "Where do you go?"

I knew what he asked but pretended not to follow him. "No Arabic," I said haughtily revving up the engine.

"No go," he shouted, showing an adequate command of a foreign language notoriously difficult to learn.

I had no inclination to take orders from a young upstart. I pushed the accelerator pedal to the floor and the car rushed forward and my tormentor jumped out of the way. Before I could let out a laugh I heard the deafening bang on the roof of the car. I braked hard and angrily turned around to see who was foolish enough to risk denting my pride and joy. Three boys in crumpled ill-fitting khakis stood there, faces red with anger, pointing guns to my head and fingers on the trigger. Suspecting that the guns were loaded I smiled sheepishly, said in perfect Arabic, "OK, you win, I go back," and turned the car around.

When I got home I received a somewhat unexpected welcome. Evelyn hugged me tight and started shedding tears of relief. A few minutes earlier, our houseboy had come running to tell her that the King had been overthrown by the army and there had been shooting near the palace. With her lively imagination, my dear wife had been picturing me surrounded by soldiers aiming their guns at my head. And worse...

3

It was quite a few years ago. Those were the good old days when I could afford to take my whole family of five for holidays to Machu Pichu and Cuzco for spiritual rejuvenation and to the Galapagos

Islands for getting back to Nature. It was the last such trip and perhaps all the more memorable for that reason alone.

On the way home we stopped in Lima for a couple of days. After an afternoon in Museo'd Oro we were infused with a new respect for antique art of Peru. I was so taken in by the artistry of everything that I saw that the idea of acquiring a couple of pieces to take home seemed quite reasonable. When I suggested this to my family, they went into a long huddle. When they came out of it, they said they will let me buy one item but there were some conditions attached. First, we will only go in a store if something in the window was worth buying. Second, the item we buy should not exceed the bonus I was expecting that year. Third, I had to carry it myself so no one could be blamed if a mishap occurred. The conditions seemed reasonable and I readily agreed. We stopped at every antique shop window for me to admire the displays of amazing variety of clay pottery and statuettes and gold ornaments. For a while dear Evelyn was rather indulgent and the kids were protesting only mildly, but it was not long before their patience began to run out. Just when five year old Anita complained of weary legs I saw an ideal item. It was a vase. It looked old, the painting on it was colourful, it was not too big or heavy to carry and it was priced within the specified limit. Every one looked at it and duly admired it, if only because they wanted my hunt to end so they could rest their aching legs in the nearby café.

Five of us noisily trooped in. We were met by a kindly middle-aged lady who asked us in rather broken English what we would like to see. When I pointed out the vase in the window, the lady put on soft gloves before picking it up and placing it gingerly on the display case. She went on to explain the historical and religious significance of all the paintings, occasionally stopping to look in a little book for the right word in English. Convinced of the significance of paintings, I still wanted to be sure that it was a genuine antique. She carefully lifted the vase, looked at the base and explained that the vase was recovered in an archeological excavation in 1928 near Cuzco and smuggled out by a sly workman. He sold it to a Lima industrialist. The family couldn't decide on who should inherit the vase, so it was put up for sale. It was one of the pair found at the site. The other was in a national museum in Europe, the lady did not recall exactly where. Albania, suggested my cheeky teenager. The lady disregarded the suggestion with enviable dignity.

Having been brought up in India, haggling for the best price is my second nature. I usually succeed in getting mangoes cheaper at Safeway by convincing the manager that they are past their best, dine free in restaurants by complaining that it was served too cold, get appliances reduced at Home Depot because the box is damaged and the appliance may be scratched. I was not going to buy an antique in a Peruvian store at the stated price of $9,999. I took out my gloves from the back pack, examined the vase closely, pointed out a couple of places where the paint had faded and asked for a proof that it was a genuine antique. The lady was dumbstruck; no one had ever asked for such a proof; price was the sufficient proof. In any event, who would believe the letter from a thief saying where he stole it from. I gently put the vase down and after the lady had finished her explanation, offered her $5,001. The lady heard my offer and collapsed into a chair. There was total silence for one full minute. Then the lady went into a detailed diatribe telling us that she was not selling cheap artifacts made in a slum by untrained craftsmen but genuine priceless finds in excavations by archeologists of international renown. The reputation of her firm was the proof that every article in that six story building was as genuine as those displayed in the Victoria and Albert Museum in London. However, considering how pretty and well-behaved the kids were, she would discount it to $9,500.

I was not impressed by the tiny discount. I went into the detailed calculation of risk I was taking of possible damage in travel, possibility of 50% customs duty when I got home and how a weak Canadian currency made American dollars so expensive. And to show my good faith I improved my offer to 5,500 causing another mini collapse. She said with great emphasis that we were wasting our time, if that is the best I could do I should take my kids to a café for a much needed drink. I was discouraged but being an old hand at this game was not quite ready to give up. So I raised my bid by a whopping $1500. I said with some humility that the vase was fabulous and certainly worth what they were asking for but $7,000 is all my credit card would take and I had run out of cash. She believed me and took pity on my situation. She accepted my offer and phoned her boss for approval which she said was a mere formality. However, from the explosion at the other end it became clear that it was not a formality. Soon, an elderly man came out of an office leaning on a cane and walked as quickly as he could to the vase. He looked at it and screamed in a high pitched voice, "Who said the price was in dollars? It is in thousand pesos, as is everything everywhere in Peru." This was news to me but it was his store, he could price his antiques any way he liked. However, it doubled the price, since a thousand pesos were worth two dollars. The old man looked at my consternation and gently offered to accept the price of 7,500,000 pesos for the vase. I could charge my credit card limit and he would accept a cheque for the balance which was against the Peruvian law but he would handle the cops if it came to that. By now every one in the family was losing patience with me and wanted to leave quickly with or without the wretched vase. Well, I was not prepared to leave without the vase. I handed him my card, got the book out and wrote the cheque. The lady packed the vase and handed it to me with a Mona Lisa smile and the best wishes for a safe journey back.

I cuddled the vase as if it was a baby every minute of the long journey back home. I unpacked it even before I had a cup of tea. The relief of all family members on finding it whole was palpable. It now sits proudly on the shelf above the fireplace and its appearance becomes a little more antique every time we light the fire.

4

In every survey that I have seen, Vancouver is rated as one of the best two or three cities in the world, whether to live in or to visit. It should not surprise anybody although, being modest Canadians, we don't expect praise for what we have. The city is our beachhead to the Pacific Ocean. The coastline is literally one superb beach after the other where you can swim, sunbathe or just watch beautiful people doing what they do best - look beautiful. If you are not an ocean person, just look the other way, ski slopes and hiking trails of glorious Whistler are only an hour away by car. The eateries in the city serve delicious food from around the world. The bars welcome you to stay and imbibe your favourite drink all night; but please, no smoking. If you are a sophisticate who must have his cigar with the brandy, please do it on the sidewalk standing in a quiet corner.

With millions of tourists, business persons, visiting dignitaries and conferees pouring in by air, land and sea, the city needs a vast array of hotels. Thankfully, there are hundreds of them; Hilton, Westin, Holiday Inn, Days' Inn and Knights' Inn, you name it. Whatever your price range, you will find a hotel. And if you can't afford even the cheapest hotel, nights are not too cold most of the year for a snooze on the beach. The reputation of Vancouver also attracts many who come to stay permanently with high expectations. However, a few newcomers find that various union regulations keep them out of jobs and government regulations out of the welfare system. Eventually, necessity drives these unfortunate individuals to roam about the city all day, collecting cans and bottles from garbage bins or sidewalks. They take these to the recycling depot to trade them for money and buy barely enough food for survival.

The area of English Bay is located next to world renowned Stanley Park and is very popular with joggers, cyclists and walkers of all ages. Comfortable benches are placed beside the paths for people to sit down, rest their feet and recover the breath. During the night, these benches serve as beds for people who fell through the cracks for one reason or the other.

Sylvia Hotel is a historic building located across the road from English Bay. The restaurant in the hotel commands a glorious view of the ocean and serves excellent food at reasonable prices. During our recent stay in the hotel, my wife and I had just finished a lovely breakfast of bacon and fried eggs with Earl Grey tea and were admiring the beautiful view of the deep blue ocean dotted with ships of all sizes. As our eyes drifted towards the beach, a circular bundle on one of the benches caught our eyes as it started shaking. Soon it became elliptical, then linear. A head popped out and then a hand slid out from the side. Eyes got a thorough rubbing, and the person stretched to his full length, and then sat up facing the ocean.

Evelyn loves a cup of coffee when she wakes up. I couldn't resist the chance of scoring some brownie points by reminding her of this service that I often provide and suggested that the unbundled gentleman might appreciate a cup of wake up coffee. She agreed that it was a wonderful idea but did not volunteer to take it to him. Now I had no choice other than delivering the coffee myself. I got a disposable cup from the waiter, filled it with coffee from the jug at the counter, added cream and two spoons of sugar to provide enough calories to get the blood pumping in a semi-frozen body. I took the hot cup out of the hotel and across the street, shifting the hot cup from one hand to the other. By now, our friend had got up and had arranged all his worldly possessions at two ends of a hockey stick carefully poised on his right shoulder. I caught up with him and the following conversation ensued.

"Will you care for a hot cup of coffee?"

"Oh, I would love it. Can you spare change for me to buy some?"

"Better still, I have brought it for you."

"Great, does it have cream?"

"Yes, enough for coffee to match the colour of my skin."

He looked at my brown Indian skin with some suspicion and did not stretch his hand for the cup which was getting too hot to hold much longer without juggling from hand to hand.

"Great, did you add any sugar?"

"Yes, two good spoonfuls, enough to take the bitterness off."

"I only take one sugar, if at all. Two spoons of sugar are bad for the teeth and worse for the weight."

"You are so skinny you could do with some weight. As for teeth, I don't see many."

"Oh, in that case it doesn't make any difference."

He plucked the coffee from my hand, fell back on the bench, impatiently took the lid off and took a long satisfying sip. Then the words seemed to slip out of his mouth, "Emma, wish I could tell you how much I miss you!"

I quietly slipped away not wishing to break his reverie.

5

Evelyn and I flew two thousand miles to Chicago to watch the *Ring Cycle* of Wagner. We thought we were being foolhardy till we met fanatics who had come all the way from Los Angeles, Belgium, Alaska, and Australia. From looks of some in the audience, they may even have come from other planets; but we were too tactful to ask. Some of the visitors had already seen these four operas more than a hundred times but were dying for more. At $800 per seat, travel and hotel expenses, and at least a week away from work, this is an expensive hobby; cynics may call it an addiction. As one addict said, "It may not be cheaper than cocaine but it is definitely more enjoyable." At seventeen hours for four operas, the effect of a shot does last longer and the hangover is not as bad. Hush during the performance suggests that the stupor induced by the drug is deeper. Huge din at the end of each Act of the opera confirms the sudden bursts of jollity greater than that due to any illicit drug. If you, dear reader, are wondering why the *Ring Cycle* and other Wagner operas make otherwise intelligent and successful people behave like zombies, here is a possible explanation.

Most operas are created by a team. One person comes up with an idea suitable for the opera and sketches a plot for the story. Another takes the plot and writes the libretto, that is, converts it into poetry. Now the person who gets all the credit for creation steps in and sets the libretto to music. A director then takes over and creates the vision of how it will all look on stage. There must be an entrepreneur to put food on the table of these creators. And finally, a producer must find the opera house, assemble the team of actors, lighting, ballet, set and costume designers, stage hands, and hustle every one to open the show on time after a minimum number of rehearsals. Although, the performance dates are set years in advance, personnel and facilities are available for only a few short weeks. Yet, the illusion of reality on stage must be complete.

Wagner's operas are different from other operas. The creator - yes, there was only one - was a genius like no other before him or since. He conceived his operas, all thirteen he created, wrote the stories, set them in poetic language appropriate for each story, composed the music which sounds like nothing he could have heard till he played it, raised the money, built an opera house and produced the operas – all by himself. When *Ring Cycle*, the set of four operas, pardon me – an introduction that lasts two and a half hours without a break, and three four and a half hour operas not counting time for two intermissions in each - were performed in 1876, everybody who was anybody in Europe was there and was mesmerized by what they saw. The influence of Wagner on all art forms is unprecedented. He impacted on the philosophy of Nietzsche, on novels of Thomas Mann and Hermann Hesse, and needless to say, on the music of every composer who followed. For 130 years since then, Wagner operas have also provided a comfortable living to generations of scalpers.

Wagner is both the most revered and the most reviled of all artists. His lifestyle left much to be desired but his art has much to desire. Some people can't tolerate Wagner because he was an anti-Semite, not just because it was the fashion of the day, but because he deeply felt that the Jews were controlling the German art scene to the exclusion of others. He was a prolific writer and published essays on every topic under the sun, most still in print. His anti-Semitic fulminations were published in various journals over a period of forty years along with essays discussing the state of German art, the art of conducting, the music of Beethoven, the state of politics in Europe, you name it. His anti-Semitic outpourings apparently did not disturb contemporary Jews. Jewish moneylenders freely lent him money, with little hope of repayment, for his lavish lifestyle. Jewish authors, impresarios, actors and composers of his time admired his operas and actively participated in them. The greatest Wagner conductors over the generations were and are of Jewish origin; Hermann Levy, Gustav Mahler, Bruno Walter, Leonard Bernstein and James Levine, to name a few. The reason is not complex. Wagner kept his personal prejudices out of his art. His operas are about human virtues and foibles. But any suggestion that virtuous characters are Aryan and villains Jews is not justified by the libretto or the music. Critics who believe that Wagner's villains represent Jews, as if only Jews can be evil, do not show much respect for Jews. Wagner had been dead for fifty years when Hitler used his works for Nazi propaganda while suppressing those of Jewish composers. It is a pity that misuse of great works of art by a crazy and destructive man has deprived many in two generations from enjoying them. It is interesting to note that Jews not only head the list of donors in Wagner programs, they are by far the largest component of the audience as well as the performers.

Another reason for coolness to Wagner's music is that his operas don't have arias like French and Italian operas do. The musical interludes and captivating scenes are long and not suited as infill on radio programs. Therefore, although people hear and hum so much Wagner-derived music from films, they don't hear much which is attributed to him. Wagner sounds different than the music of other composers of eighteenth and nineteenth centuries. The implication of this difference is that many people familiar with Mozart and Beethoven find Wagner strange. Conversely, once one becomes familiar with Wagner, other music starts sounding somewhat tame. Furthermore, Wagner operas are long. The acts in some Wagner operas are longer than many other complete operas. They need large orchestras, big casts and elaborate sets and therefore are expensive to stage. Consequently, they are only performed by major houses and seats are priced at a premium. A six hour long performance with big ticket price scares all but diehard Wagnerites. However, there is no shortage of them. Operas are sold out months in advance and often a substantial donation to the opera house is advised to secure the high-price seats. No wonder, in spite of their stupor, the druggies are hard to please.

There is a strict code the audience must follow. Violators risk being lynched. By code I do not mean dress, although almost every one dresses as if they are "going to the opera." The code is about what you do and don't do when the lights are dimmed in the hall. It was Wagner who started the custom of dark halls. He did it to minimize distractions and to promote respect for his art. You must be in your seat before the lights dim unless you want to spend the Act cooling your heels in the lobby. Once in your seat, you can fall asleep if you wish as long as you do not snore. You do not disrupt the continuity by clapping or cheering after the soprano has moved you in a difficult passage. You are encouraged to scream your heart out when the curtain finally comes down at the end of an Act, but if you do it at the end of a scene, the concierge will escort you to the lobby if only to save your life. You do not rustle your program, zip and unzip your handbag, cough or sneeze but you may breathe so long you do it quietly. For heaven's sake, don't whisper any comment, favourable or otherwise, unless you want the audience around you to hiss you to shame. If your cell phone goes off, I am afraid it will be worse than the conflagration at the end of *"The Twilight of the Gods"* and the rest of the audience will treat you with contempt for the rest of the week. To summarise the code, you can take in the performance, everything else is strictly *verboten*.

As if to prove that a Wagner opera is not just entertainment but also serious business, most opera houses offer seminars, pre-opera talks and in one case post-opera talks at midnight. Just like the operas, seminars and talks are sold out events. The public is not allowed to ask questions. The practice of audience participation stopped after a renowned speaker dropped dead with exhaustion after taking more questions than he could answer. However, several groups spontaneously form in the hallways for agitated discussions till security guards send them away to the nearest Starbucks.

With all the seminars, pre- and post-opera talks, start time of six and final curtain at midnight, one needs a well-thought out strategy to last the week without being escorted out for some minor misdemeanor like snoring. The plan for the day should take the individual's physical capacity into consideration. Early-to-bed types need an afternoon nap while late-in-bed types should spend the afternoon leisurely studying the libretto. When setting the alarm clock to wake them up, the nappers must make allowances for slow service at early dinner in the restaurant, late taxi, busy traffic and line-ups at the coat check and washroom. A good sleep every night is mandatory. A day on your feet at the museum or art gallery may seem like a good idea because you would be on your seat all evening, but it could lead to the brain being switched off just when you need it most, that is, when the person in the next seat asks what you thought of the soprano. The transportation after the opera is critical. It can be a long wait for the cab when a thousand cabs need to be launched but only one is available. That is why the hotel near the opera house can charge several hundred dollars per night for a comfortable bed and little else, and is fully booked for the season. It is advisable to travel a couple of days before the first event and to plan a quiet week after the operas to get back on one's feet.

Thanks to careful planning, we had great fun in Chicago. We have already started saving for our next Wagner vacation. We look forward to meeting you there, wherever "there" is.

6

Chicago is a bustling city located on the west shore of Lake Michigan. Michigan Avenue is the hub of activity – particularly tourist activity. Lakeshore Boulevard is the only road to the east of Michigan Avenue. Grant Park, located between the two roads, separates the lake from the buildings in the city. Congress Road is a short east-west connector for the two roads. Among other things, Chicago is famous for its art and architecture. Chicago Symphony Orchestra and Lyric Opera offer performances superior to those anywhere else. There are countless art galleries full of major art works of the last millennium from all over the world. Architectural gems of last century are found on every block. Almost every cross road has statues whose pictures adorn the halls of middle class homes of America. The intersection of Congress and Michigan is an exception, if only because it has three statues, not just one. Two double-sized sandstone statues of Indian warriors adorn each side of Grant. The warriors, on magnificent horses, face each other. One is shooting an arrow and the other hurling a rock, hopefully not at each other. Third statue is a brass figure of a young woman in human size placed on a bed of daffodils on the divider on Grant. She is wearing a tight dress with flaring skirt that supports the statue. Excitement is clearly visible on her beautiful face. Her hair is loose, blowing backwards in the wind. Her hands are stretched out as if exhorting the passing traffic. As if to avoid the arrows and rocks from the warriors she is placed a little west of the line of two horses.

I was impressed more by the lady than the warriors, probably because I am an Indian too, although of a different variety. I made numerous inquiries but no one seemed to know who the lady was, how she got there and what, if anything, she was doing there. Tour guide smoothly moved on to a different subject when asked. Not even the hotel doorman who faced her most of the day would hazard a guess. I couldn't hold my curiosity and asked every local I came across and finally the Publicity Manager of Lyric Opera who was attending a seminar with me. The opera is currently doing Wagner's Ring cycle in which Brunnhilde is woken up by her prince after a long sleep. His answer made sense. He assured me that Opera doesn't know how the statue got there, not even who the sculptor is. But they do believe that it is an artist's vision of Brunnhilde greeting the sun on waking up.

"Why is she facing west, if she is greeting the sun," I asked.

"She is facing the city." He replied and added, "When was the last time a soprano sang her best line with back to the audience?"

Indeed, a good actor always faces the audience when delivering her best lines. In America, even statues are on stage.

7

It was the day to leave Chicago, albeit reluctantly. I packed and had a rather hearty American breakfast. I still had a couple of hours to kill before heading for the airport. My hotel was located near Lake Michigan and Grant Park. It was a beautiful sunny morning, typical of this gorgeous city, I was told, and it made sense to take a walk in the park and use up the excess calories from that stack of pancakes and Aunt Jemima's sugary syrup. I had read in a pamphlet in the hotel lobby that the views of the skyline are something to behold from the south end of the park. So, I headed south at a slow pace examining various statues for which the park is justly renowned.

I reached the south end of the park in about three quarters of an hour. As I came out of a clump of trees and climbed up to the road level, a huge vertical wall of a magnificent building rose in front of me. The wall was decorated by enormous paintings of a young man and a young woman, both really handsome. I wondered if they were movie stars and out of curiosity stopped a middle-aged couple who were strolling towards me. The following conversation followed.

I: "Sorry to bother you both. Could you please tell me who the people in the paintings on the wall are?"

The gentleman: "You must be the only person on this planet who does not know that couple, or are you after something?"

I: "Sorry sir. I am from a small town in India. We don't get foreign films there and I don't know much about your stars."

The gentleman, in exasperation: "They are not stars. They are John and Jackie Kennedy."

I: "Thank you sir. Why are they famous?"

49

The lady: "Jack Kennedy, President Kennedy, don't you know?"

I: "Sorry madam, I thought Mr. Bush was the President."

The gentleman: "Mr. Bush is the President. Mr. Kennedy was President from 1961 to 1963."

I: "Oh, that long ago. He must have done something great."

The lady: "He was very popular, probably the most popular President ever."

I: "Thank you for telling me this, madam. Did he become popular because he led your great country to victory in a major war?"

The gentleman: "No, he did not. Actually he started a war which divided the country, cost us a great deal and we lost after ten years."

I: "Sorry to hear that sir. Perhaps he brought great prosperity to the people!"

The lady: "No, he did not do that either."

I: "Then why did your people love him so much madam? He must have done something!"

The gentleman: "Well, he did make great speeches exhorting Americans to put the country ahead of themselves."

I: "He must have been a great orator and writer!"

The lady: Oh! He was not. He had a strange Boston accent and other people wrote his speeches."

I: "Well sir, madam, I am confused. Why do Americans worship him so?"

The lady: "He was handsome and rich."

The gentleman: "She was young, beautiful and also rich."

Both: "Isn't that enough?"

I: "Indeed it is. I now know what makes Americans great. Thank you for explaining it to me."

The gentleman, softly: "Oh! And he was shot by an assassin, like Abraham Lincoln."

I felt distracted. I looked at my watch and starting walking briskly towards my hotel.

8

A funny thing happened a few years ago. We were on a cycling holiday in the south of France. The tour operator had provided the bicycles and we had taken minimum personal effects with us, only what we could paddle on the uphill. There were ten of us, including the guide. The guide was a petite French Canadian equally at home in English and French and therefore well qualified for the leadership of the Liberal party of Canada. The routine was the same every day. We got up with the sun and had the breakfast of delicious bread and nourishing cheese with strong coffee. We rode for a couple of hours to another picturesque village where we stopped to replenish our bodies with bread, cheese and coffee. Then ride to another village for lunch of more bread, cheese and coffee followed by two more riding sessions with a bread, cheese and coffee interval in another beautiful spot. To paraphrase Tolstoy, every village was beautiful in the same way but it was different in the taste of its bread, cheese and coffee. However, by the dinner time, the tired and hungry riders were ready for more variety. We found it when the local wine was poured before the dinner and the bread and cheese were only the side dishes. The happy hour was followed by an excellent dinner with many courses which were served with decent interval in between for copious consumption of wine. By the time the dessert arrived we were nicely inebriated and didn't really care what it was.

After so many years, I do not remember much about the conversation, either among us or with the waitresses who were invariably pretty. There were a couple of gentlemen in our group who attempted to charm these ladies into more than serving the food and drink. But, with rare exceptions, the overtures were

51

turned down with a sweet smile. Even when they were successful, a curtain of discretion was drawn over them to avoid the trouble with wives at home.

We were in a particularly boisterous mood during our last dinner. We were dining in a large and pretentious restaurant rather than small village eateries we had become accustomed to. Elegantly dressed men with superior airs served us with disdain that Europeans have for North Americans. They looked down even more on me because, thanks to the deaf ear for different tongues, my French was still non-existent. The waiter couldn't hide his disgust when I ordered Beef Wellington rather than Duck Napoleon which more diplomatic customers were ordering.

After the courses of soup, salad and palate cleanser helped on their way down by numerous glasses of wine, the dinner arrived. As one should have expected in a respectable French establishment, Duck Napoleon was served first. It was a large serving of white and brown slices of meat in the centre of a huge plate, surrounded by a ring of vegetables chosen for their colours as well as taste. Watching them being served to ladies on both sides did wonders for my appetite. I now anxiously waited for my Beef Wellington. However, the waiters had other business to attend to and did not pay heed to my eagerness. Other diners were almost finished when my dinner arrived. The plate had a sparkling silver bell-shaped lid over it, presumably keeping the food hot. It was placed in front of me with great ceremony, fit for the beef being served to Lord Wellington in a victory celebration. Then the waiter lifted the lid. I eagerly looked at the plate under a puff of steam. It was indeed the same size as other plates. However, it only had a tiny piece of beef placed in the centre with four thin slices of zucchini artistically placed around it. There was a drop of the chef's famous sauce on the side of beef which less sharp eyes would have missed. I was disappointed in the serving, certain that it was not going to do much for my rumbling stomach. However, I hoped that the taste will justify the price and the pomp with which it was presented.

I was chewing the bite which was beef when the waiter asked with a smirk one could see from a mile away, "How did you find the beef, sir?"

Oh, his English is not as bad as he has been pretending, I thought before replying, "Purely by accident, as I turned over the zucchini."

The laughter around the table echoed in the room for quite some time and the snooty waiter was not seen again for the rest of the evening.

9

It was a beautiful morning in Calgary earlier this month when Evelyn and I drove to Banff. There we joined a group of 65 sturdy men and women. Some of the group were in their sixties like me but most were younger. The group was headed for a one-week hiking camp in Banff National Park. I hadn't hiked much since I left India forty years ago. However; I was hoping on this trip to get in touch with my inner self by communing with pristine nature. Two buses took us on a one-hour journey to the trailhead at appropriately named Mosquito Creek. The luxurious buses were thoughtfully equipped with toilet facilities so important to the backcountry visitors.

It had been raining heavily in Mosquito Creek for a while but it did not deter us. With packs on our backs and songs on our lips we trudged through muddy trails and shaky one-log bridges on torrential streams traversing twelve kilometres in five hours. We arrived at the camp thoroughly exhausted, very wet and not a little frightened by the thunder and lightning. After so much exertion it was a relief to see all the tents holding up to the stormy conditions. The dinner tent was particularly welcoming with herbal tea and unsalted crackers. An adventurous week was in front of us, though not in the way we had imagined at the time of booking for the trip.

It continued to rain cats and dogs for the next two days, with sprinklings of hail and occasional snow. Only the toughest few of the group braved the inclement weather and poor trail conditions to go on hikes. The rest stayed in tents and read their books or gathered in the dining tent to play games. I teamed up with three retired English teachers to play Scrabble. After losing twice, I demanded a 50 points handicap because English was my second language. Other players turned this down with scorn. In a huff, I joined the Bridge set and promptly lost a bundle.

Two and a half days of continuous rain affected people differently. Macho types took it in their stride. But some got depressed and one or two even started hallucinating. One big burly bear of a man spent the night shivering in fear that there was a bear growling near his tent. Just before dawn, when it was too late to go back to sleep, he realised, with as much relief as annoyance, that the growl was a rather loud snoring in the next tent.

I attempted to inject humour in this grim situation, but these attempts misfired. Other campers started avoiding me fearing my "twisted" sense of humour. It all started with Andy. He was a mountain goat on a hike and the official camp doctor at other times. I asked him whether I could go with him on a particularly tough hike because it would be nice to be with a doctor if I twisted my ankle. His response conveyed all the contempt a good hiker has for a novice who had not dared out of camp for two days of thunder and lightning. "Staying in the camp is the best protection from injuries", the good doctor prescribed. In spite of this rebuff I continued my attempts to humour the group. Guido, a young social worker spent an amusing hour that afternoon taking note of my views on the state of the human race. Later in the dinner queue, after making sure of being within hearing of Guido, I warned a camper in his sixties that this young man was collecting data on how old people coped with vicissitudes of their lives and will probably interview him too. Needless to say Guido also felt that my humour was a bit odd. The last straw was on my first hike the next day. The leader took a wrong turn and we found ourselves very close to the highway where the bus had dropped us on the first day. Looking quite serious I suggested that we should hitch hike to Banff rather than struggle back to camp. This attempt at humour finally sealed the group's impression of my weirdness. For rest of the week I was made to feel like an Indian from a lowly trader family in the presence of holy Brahmins.

I shared the tent with a doctor who kindly shares her life with me and a couple made up of an engineer wife and a lawyer husband. Just before I went to sleep, may even be after I dozed off, I heard them discussing their professions. It must be the deluge of the last sixty hours that led their thoughts to the stories in the Bible, the origin of the universe and the purpose of life. After discussing at some length how their respective professions influence their views on these important matters, the discussion turned into a banter about whose profession was the oldest.

Evelyn got out of the gate first. "Why of course, medicine is the oldest. On the sixth day of Creation God operated on Adam to remove the rib and create Eve. He acted as a surgeon - though without a license - and therefore medicine must be the first profession.

The other member of the gentler sex was not about to give in. "Why," she said, "On the first day God created the universe out of chaos. Surely, this was an engineering feat and you must accept Engineering as the older profession."

The lawyer lay there smiling vaguely and looking at the mosquitoes hovering near the lamp. At last his wife got annoyed and asked, "What are you smiling about? Why don't you say something?"

After a suitably long pause the lawyer murmured, "Who created the chaos in the first place?"

A heavy sigh from the wife suggested that a new chaos was on the way.

## 10

My wife and I returned to Greece after thirty years, this time with our daughters Roshan and Anita. Kostas was our travel agent. He had arranged a wonderful ten day tour of mainland Greece, a week in a suburb of Athens for Olympic events and two weeks in the islands. For our tour and stay in the distant suburb, we rented a small car which had to be returned at the agency at the airport a day before we were to leave for the islands. Kostas offered to help us return the car, store our extra luggage during the two weeks we were in the islands, and take us to our overnight hotel in Athens. Every element of the arrangement had been gone through with a fine-tooth comb and approved. But the gods hadn't had their say yet.

Kostas arrived at our suburban hotel in his van at the appointed hour. He proudly showed its gleaming exterior and spotless interior. Then he announced with certain pride that he had owned it for thirty years to the day and looked after it better than his family. The van had survived the notorious Athens traffic without a scratch. He serviced it himself from head to tail every month and changed the oil before it had a speck of dirt in it. The van was washed more often than some members of his family: it had cost money to acquire and it helped grease the wheels of his business unlike the members of the family who only talked to him when they needed help.

The van was loaded with our cases which were to be left in his care. The bags we were to carry to the islands were in the trunk of our car. While arranging the bags I noticed a fire extinguisher. I could not imagine why one would carry one in the car but the law required it; a large notice on the inside of the trunk said so. The reason for the law was not hard to find. Greeks were avid smokers but they hated the sight of cigarette stubs. The only thing to be done when the lighted end had reached the finger tips was to flick it out of the car with great panache. Once in a while it landed in the passing car and the consequences were not pretty. Hence the law requiring a fire extinguisher in every car. I did not believe we could become the butt of such joke by the fate and arranged bags all over the extinguisher and the plastic bag containing the control valve.

We drove to the airport, Kostas in his van and our family of four in our car behind him. Driving in Greece needs sharp reactions and nerves of steel. The machismo of Greeks is expressed behind the wheel and takes full flight when they see a young woman driving the car ahead. Roshan was giving full rein to her fiery temper by the time the bustle of Athens traffic was left behind and we were on a six lane rather deserted airport road. This super highway was built to accommodate the speedy traffic of Olympic Committee members between the airport and their luxury hotels. Kostas picked up speed and we reluctantly followed suit. Soon the speedometer was hitting 150 km. The exhilaration of speed took hold of us but Kostas was no doubt used to it. It was at the height of our excitement when Roshan noticed flames coming out of the back of the van. Kostas was, however, totally unaware of them. Roshan hooted the horn and tried to get along the van to warn him. But there was no way a Greek male was going to let a young Canadian woman pass him. He speeded as well and hooted back. After a long minute or so of this drama, a Mercedes 500SL saw the writing on the wall, sped past Kostas and waved him to stop.

It was at this moment that Kostas saw the flames of fury from his well-serviced van. He stopped on the wide shoulder and Roshan parked carefully at a safe distance behind him. He ran to the back of the van and started to pull our cases out. My wife screamed telling him to run to safety and not worry about the cases while I screamed about the safety of the contents. But he continued pulling the cases with one hand while fighting the flames with the other.

The incredible scene came to a sudden end. Anita had the presence of mind to think of the extinguisher in our car. She found it in the jumble of bags, located and fitted the control valve and rushed with the red cylinder blazing to attack the flames with the zeal of a novice fire fighter. It didn't matter that Kostas was getting as much of the extinguishing foam as the flames; he deserved it for being in the way. The flames did get enough foam to subside and quickly died without a murmur. We all breathed a sigh of relief. Kostas looked at the damage and the worried frown was replaced by a heavenly smile, "The damage is superficial, small leak from pipe connecting gas tank to engine, will be fixed in no time and the van will be good for another thirty years." However, he was not ready to drive the van till the leak was fixed. He arranged for a tow truck and we drove to the airport car rental. The ride to the hotel on the new train may not have been as comfortable as the van but it felt safer, even though I had my pocket picked.

Next morning we took a short plane ride to Santorini. We spent four glorious days in heaven and took a hovercraft to the island of Crete. It was 10:30 PM when we checked in at the hotel after a six hours voyage on a cushion of air. As soon as I had put the cases down, Evelyn, who had been studying the tourist guide, screamed with delight, "This is something we have to do - a 16 km hike along a gorge in rugged mountains, starting at 1000 meters ASL and dropping to sea level. Legend has it that this trail was taken by Alexander the Great on his great march to India and one can still see the hoof marks on the rocks, although there is some question about which ones are from Great man's horse. We must do this hike to get the flavour of Crete. I will call the receptionist and get the details."

There was only one possible date for this trip during our four day stay in Crete - the next day. A bus would pick us up at 6 AM, take us to the start point 250 km away and pick us up at the other end of the trail. Expected arrival of 9 PM seemed to me a little early considering the distances but not after the good wife reminded me how Greeks drove their buses. In any event, the details depressed me but not the others. My athletic daughters said that they needed exercise and supported their mother. Looking back, it may only have been out of gender solidarity and the wish to teach old fat scrooge a lesson. The receptionist wanted to know within next 23 seconds if we wanted to be on the bus. We rushed down the stairs three steps at a time, paid 300 Euros cash for our transportation and we were booked. As soon as the die was cast, stomachs growled, not only for dinner, but for next day's breakfast and lunch as well. Dinner at midnight fitted right in with the local custom. I stealthily pocketed some bread for breakfast and we bought some peaches for lunch from a stall which was ready to call it a night.

After a four hour sleep, we were up and raring to go at the hotel door at six o'clock sharp. A minibus showed up half hour late and took us to a gathering point next to a garbage dump we could smell but not see in the dark. We waited for the bus on the side of a busy road. A double-decker bus showed up in another half hour. We climbed up and found three seats separated by several rows. The guide introduced herself via the microphone in Greek, German, French and Italian and informed us that there was no W.C. (wash room, if you insist) on the bus but there was a stop in three hours for stretch, smoke and coffee. There were many groans but no one dared to complain to the guide. The bus did stop every few minutes but only to pick up would-be hikers. Soon, the bus was bursting at the seams, like many of its passengers, but driver and the guide took no notice and the passengers minded their own business – holding on till the W.C. stop.

Eventually the bus stopped at a convenience store, not a minute too soon considering the dash of passengers to the W.C. Relieved hikers had rather late breakfast and bought lunch. Some people noticed that the guide kept a close watch on how much was spent by each hiker and surreptitiously pocketed a bundle from the store owner when we had boarded the bus. We got to the start point where we paid five euros each to enter the national park and begin the hike. I claimed my senior's discount but was gruffly brushed aside – discount is only for European Community citizens. The guide told us, again in four languages – none intelligible – expected arrival times at check points. The most crucial was the arrival at the beach before 6:00 PM when a ferry will take us to the bus a couple of kilometers along the rugged coast. Seven hours for sixteen kilometers downhill is a stroll for the fit and rested, young at heart and body. My family took off in great spirits. For this jet-lagged overweight Canadian who had missed his sleep for the last few nights and was not used to blinding sun and scorching heat, it was like a marathon race in hell with no end in sight. "Pace yourself, old man, you can do it," I told myself. Soon I was the huffing and puffing tail in this group of sixty intrepid hikers from fifty countries.

It was a picturesque setting of lovely mountains - green, not the white I am used to in Canada. I am told that it got prettier as the gorge got deeper and when the red cliffs started appearing. Some hikers with sharp eyes and lively imagination noticed hoof marks and could tell from the shape when they were made by Alexander's great horse. But I was panting too hard to notice. When I stopped, it was to recover my breath, hydrate myself, and wipe the sweat off my bald head, brows and glasses. There was no time to waste on appreciating scenery. I had to stay with rest of the group so as not to get lost in the woods

The examples of Greek entrepreneurship were everywhere. A couple of men waited at regular intervals with their donkeys to give rides, for a modest fee of thirty euros, to hikers who got injured or disheartened. I was sorely tempted, but I am too much of a cheap skate to part with that much money. At every point of rock fall warning, there was a young man with a steel helmets with horns, just like those Valkyrie helmets in Wagner operas, to rent them to you for a euro each. At the end of rock fall zone his colleague collected the helmets and rented them to clients coming the other way. You paid the rent at each rock fall zone and by the end of the hike you had parted with ten precious euros.

Just when I was running out of steam and starting to drag myself on all fours, my lonely brain cells became activated. I realized that unless I picked up speed, I would barely make the boat and miss out on dinner set for 5:30. The thought of being rocked and rolled for five hours or more on the boat and the bus on a protesting stomach was all I needed to get the second wind. I started walking as if I was in the Himalayas in my young days forty years ago. I did the last five kilometers in an hour and joined the family at the stipulated dining room in good time to refresh myself before ordering moussaka and Greek salad with extra olive oil. The food of ancient Greek gods made me feel like Atlas without the world on his back. There was spring in my feet when I walked on to the boat and again from the boat to the bus.

The spring lost its elasticity by the time bus dropped us at the garbage dump emitting unusual odours. A minibus picked us up after the mandatory half hour wait and dropped us at the hotel at midnight. When I asked the receptionist about the discrepancy in the time of return with what she had told us the previous night, she shrugged her shoulders and walked away. We decided that this Cretan and courtesy do not cohabit and went to bed to snore and dream of a sumptuous breakfast buffet which, alas, remained a dream.

11

Evelyn used to suffer from frequent attacks of migraines. Much though I sympathized with her, I still managed to cause her grief. There was always that ray of blinding light as I opened the door to get out of the bedroom, the squeak of the shoe when I crept from one basement room to the other, the wail of the armchair spring as I shifted my weight, the clatter of the lid on the saucepan when I boiled an egg for dinner, the hiss of the kettle in making the cup of tea. The list of my actions that jabbed her unbearably painful head with stabs from the devil incarnate is long and inexhaustible. For a long time, my empathy for her was somewhat limited. I had never suffered a headache in my life and could never quite feel the suffering she went through. She often said, only half in jest, that I never had a headache because I only had one neuron in my brain and a lot of empty space. The lonely neuron had all the room for its orbiting and had nothing to collide with to jar the brain. I always knew that her brain was loaded with neurons – her academic and professional success was proof if one were needed. This only added weight to her theory on the origin of migraines.

My life of headache-ignorant bliss ended on a trip to the Gold Coast. We were driving back from the hinterland to the capital city when it grew dark. The roads were more potholes than tarmac and did not have guardrails to protect nervous foreigners from driving off into fathomless ditches when attacked by headlights of onrushing trucks. Our urge to use the return portion of our ticket in this life, rather than the next, induced us to stop for the night in the only hotel of a small town. We were uncomfortable at the thought of sleeping in the bed offered us. We were even more uncomfortable in it. Thankfully, the sun rose early and we were out of bed and into the car before the cocks had woken up too many truck drivers. We got to the capital of this great country safely enveloped in sound; the sound of snoring passengers. We checked into a luxury hotel and hopped into a comfortable bed to make up for the horrors of the night. It wasn't long before we were soundlessly asleep.

All good things come to an end but not as unpleasantly as the bliss in a comfortable bed in the Gold Coast. I woke up with a start with a feeling I had never had in my life of six decades plus. My head felt as if it was ready to split in two. My body felt as if it was being tossed about in furious waves of the ocean one could see through the translucent curtains on the window. I screamed to my bedmate that she was shaking the bed and causing me no end of grief. She woke up, rubbed her eyes, shaking the bed even harder and asked what was wrong with me. I screamed that my head was bursting as if my brain was going to jump out like a cat from the window of a burning house and she was making things worse by all her shaking. She got up, threw me her Mona Lisa smile and said, "It seems the neuron has found company. Wonder if it laid eggs or just split into two."

I was in no shape for a fight. At least the waves were gone with the source and a serene calm had returned to bed. I fell back into the stupor for a couple of hours more. Suddenly the head cleared and I was ready to face the world. I found the inspiration of my life at the hotel travel counter. Just in time, as it turned out. She was about to cancel the return flight as I got there. She was happy to see me, though disappointed that our stay was not prolonged. A good breakfast helped her get over it and we enjoyed rest of the day near the hotel pool.

Every thing was hunky dory for our morning flight to Canada the next day. The plane took off and before long the sign to keep seat belts on went out. I pushed back my backrest and suddenly my head was ready to split again. All the misery of 24 hours ago returned in full force. Again, it lasted for two hours and then my head cleared up. Alas! It was too late for lunch. I had to make do with a bag of peanuts and coffee the hostess produced after much begging. I consoled myself that the rumbling in my poor stomach was a joy compared to the battle of neurons in my head. The rest of the journey home was uneventful, thank Heavens. After a good sleep in our own bed, we both went to work the next day as usual.

The office was anything but as usual. The desk was covered with papers to be attended to. Hundred of calls had to be returned. Large cheques needed my signature. Time went quickly. Then the secretary came in to ask if I wanted her to get me a sandwich. Suddenly I felt as if a week-old hunk of dried bread had hit my head. The headache of the last two days had returned. I screamed in pain and fell back in my chair. The secretary wondered if she had done something wrong and slipped out. I lay there in the chair for two hours. Then the head cleared just as quickly as it had clouded. I called the secretary and asked for my sandwich. She said there wasn't any because I had screamed at her rather than giving her a straight answer. She produced a cup of coffee and a cookie. That had to tide me over for rest of the day.

I duly reported my headache to Evelyn. She pushed me in the car and headed for the hospital. They gave me a bed and told me to wait for the doctor. I lay there in a hospital gown with my bare right arm lying over the sheet. Suddenly there was a shriek from the mouth I adore. She had noticed a tic bite near my elbow. The doctor rushed in when she heard the shriek, looked at the tic bite and ordered me to see the tropical disease specialist the next morning. The specialist prescribed an antibiotic and in a few days the clouds in my head dissipated never to return again.

My dear friend for life believes that her theory has been confirmed. If my lonely neuron had laid the eggs the baby neurons did not survive; if the neuron had split, it had coalesced again. Either way I have returned to my original happy state of a man with a lonely neuron in his head.

# Joys of a Doctor's Husband

## 1

It is still fresh in my mind although it happened more than twenty five years ago. I came home one evening, exhausted after a hard day's work. I was greeted by my wife, who looked after our three children full time. She was very excited. "Sit down, I got great news," she said

"Great, I am all ears."

"I am not too old for Med School."

"I didn't know you were interested in a career."

"I am, that of a doctor."

"Splendid. Did you talk to someone in the Med School?"

"Yes, I did. They said my experience of child rearing in various countries is an asset and will help me get in. All I need is a few University courses in Physics, Chemistry and Biology."

"Great. Go for it."

She took me at my word. Going for it meant Senior High courses in all these subjects to qualify for University level. One year's hard work with some emotional and tutorial support from family and friends accomplished that. Four years of science degree were followed by three years of Med School and two years of Hospital training. Ten years of unrelenting hard work qualified her as a doctor. Now there was a real doctor in the family in addition to a phony (Ph. D.) one who was sick at the sight of blood. But it took one phone call from my lawyer to prove that two doctors in the household, one too many.

I had Harry working on the reorganization of some business affairs and the deadline was fast approaching. The poor man was working long hours to get legal papers organized. One evening he called home when we were in the middle of our dinner. My teen age daughter picked up the phone and asked in an annoyed tone who the caller wanted.

"This...is...Harry...Humboldt...Is...Dr....Jain...available?" asked my lawyer in the slow speech of someone being paid by the minute.

"Which Dr. Jain?" asked my daughter, annoyed that some one will dare to call any one but her during the dinner hour?

"Beg ... your ... pardon?" the confused caller muttered.

"There are two doctors here, which one do you want?" asked the daughter.

A long silence followed. Then stammering could be heard out of the ear phone. "Hmmm, Dr. ...Sudhir ...Jain, ... please."

I took the phone, quickly settled the matter with him, apologized to the family and resumed the dinner.

At month's end, the lawyer's bill arrived. The time spent and amount charged on that phone call was highlighted by the accountant. The cost of confusion in answering the call was staring me through yellow ink and telling me in no uncertain terms, "Don't do it again, never again."

There was only one way to avoid the recurrence. That day I announced to all who would listen that this phony was reverting to being Mr. Jain. There was only one real doctor in the household and she will be the one entitled to be called Dr. Jain.

Since then, that teenager has acquired a Ph. D, another is doing an M.D. and the third is doing her D.Dent. But this doesn't cause problems. I can't afford a lawyer any more.

## 2

Evelyn is one of those young women who put all they have in whatever they do. She did that as a student and now she is doing it as a doctor. The patients' welfare is her prime, nay the only, concern. Any time of the day, any day of the week, the pager is hooked to her belt. Every patient call is duly forwarded to her pager, every page is promptly attended to. The dinner is sometimes overcooked, kids are late, even miss their soccer games, I am pulled out from urgent meetings or even worse from my study of the business page because duty calls.

Most patients are considerate and it is rare that she is woken up because a patient wants to know whether she would be in her clinic the following morning or if she could prescribe for the sore throat her husband has had for a week. Generally, the caller is sick and Evelyn is grateful for the opportunity to serve.

I am cut from a different cloth. I am the sort who concentrates on the job at hand and hates being interrupted. So much so that I never answer the phone unless it is in the half hour I assign every day for that purpose. I never turn the radio on when driving and answer all passenger queries with monosyllables in case I miss some crucial occurrence on the road. I never could understand my beloved wife's patience with her patients. I put up with it for the sake of marital harmony but the disturbance to my sleep is something that I can barely put up with. I must have six hours of sleep to refresh myself. I am a senior executive in an investment house where my colleagues have heated debates in meetings that last till all but one participant have lost their voices. Thus we arrive at the decision on which hinge the fortunes of the clients and our bonuses.

One evening I had just shut my eyes, at least that is what I felt, when I had to open them again because Evelyn was speaking with an unusual concern in her voice. Soon I discovered that the patient on the other end was feeling depressed and threatening to end her unhappy life. Evelyn was, as any kind doctor would, trying to calm her down. I listened to the conversation with growing impatience. At last I could hold it no longer.

"Ask her address," I said.

"Shhh! why?"

"I will tell you the nearest location of a bridge."

"Shut up."

"OK, ask her where her husband is."

That seemed like a good idea and Evelyn passed on the question. I groaned when I heard, "He is sleeping. He has to go to work in the morning."

The answer did not sit well with the conscientious doctor. She gently asked the patient to drop by her office in the morning, put the phone down, and went back to the sleep of the just. I tossed and turned wondering why some sleeps are more important than others.

3

To have a personal doctor looking after him full time, one has to be an invalid in the emergency ward of the hospital or a Bill Gates equivalent who is constantly followed by a doctor hired by major pension funds to protect their investment in the event of his untimely departure from the scene. I have this privilege without belonging to either extreme. It is because I am one of the lucky few who are married to a doctor. Evelyn is very well known among her colleagues for her competence and among her patients for being caring. The combination of competence and caring is not as common as you would think. That is why my doctor is so much in demand. Still, she finds time to spot any signs of trouble in me before I am even aware of it. She is so caring not because I am tall and handsome. In fact I am a short, fat, bald brownie. I have no skills to help with the household chores. I can do the dishes but I cannot cook anything edible. The last time I did the laundry, two sweaters, a necktie and a dress were ruined. That was years ago and I have not been allowed near the washing machine since.

The reason I am so valuable to the dear doctor is simple. She doesn't like to bother with money. All she wants is that her bank honours her cheques and her credit card never approaches the hateful limit. It is my job to deposit funds in her account when it is running low and pay the bills on time without incurring penalties or interest. It may look important to the uninitiated, but it pales in significance to my main claim to respect. I do have some skill, some may call it luck, in managing money and I look after the family's savings for the doctor's eventual retirement. I place our past and current savings in low risk, high yield investments. But what makes me indispensable is this. I can write but I do not like to. I keep every bit of information in my head. My head is like a filing cabinet full of valuable documents. There is no paper or electronic file to tell anyone where the money is. I reckon that if no one knows where what is, they cannot run away with it. My dear wife appreciates this argument and considers it worth the risk that, without me, she will not know where any penny is. She minimizes this risk by looking after me as well as any one can.

Two weapons of a doctor come in handy in protecting my health and wellbeing. The prescription pad is one. If traffic is bad on the way home and she looks at my ruffled demeanour, out comes her prescription pad. I pass her the pen and she hands me a sheet of paper with squiggly lines on it. I take it to my trusty pharmacist and return home with pills to be taken four times a day with a tall glass of tap water for the next two weeks. A little sniffle, another prescription and the cold is banished before arriving. Unfortunately, the pills have to be taken till the bottle is empty. The other weapon is referral to the specialist. I take time to consider before replying, I am sent for hearing tests. She

69

has trouble hearing me, I mumble, off I go to a speech therapist. She has trouble sleeping, it must be my snoring. Ear, Nose and Throat specialist, here I come. I couldn't remember a quote from Shakespeare. I got tested for Alzheimer. Luckily they found that it was not at an advanced stage yet.

If you are thinking that the man doth protest too much, you are right. Life was rather comfortable. We were empty nesters, could sleep till eight and be at work at 8:30. Then she noticed me bending over backward with a hand on my back. She had a word with her favourite physiotherapist and set up an appointment on the following day. The physio had me doing all sorts of contortions for a long time. When the allotted time had nearly run out, she told me that there was nothing seriously wrong with my back that some exercise couldn't fix. She showed me a few exercises to be done for an hour twice a day. My wife made sure that I was up at seven to work at keeping away the backache that I never had.

One day I lost my footing when getting up to get a snack. My wife noticed it. Next morning, there was a call from the physio friend. She wanted to see me in the afternoon about my knee. "What knee" I asked. "The joint between leg and thigh" she said. She told me that the doctor had noticed weakness in my knees and I had no choice in the matter.

When I got there, she told me to lie on my back. Then she moved my legs up and down, sideways, pulled, pushed, twisted clockwise and anticlockwise, had me walk slowly, then run on the spot as fast as I could. When I started dripping sweat and breathing fumes, she asked me to stop and sit down. "Nothing wrong with the knees or ankles that a little exercise can't fix" she said and handed me a pamphlet with a series of exercises. To be done morning and evening every day together with the back exercises, she advised gently but firmly. My wife looked at the exercises in the pamphlet and set the alarm for six, an hour earlier. She also made sure that I was in the exercise room at nine so I could be in bed at eleven.

## 4

I was going to hit fabulous fifty in a couple of weeks and was looking forward to a dinner of fried chicken with crispy noodles and champagne flowing freely from the bottle to my glass and then down my taste buds. For the special occasion, Evelyn decided I deserved a special present and gave it to me in a brightly coloured envelope two weeks in advance with instructions to open it the same day. It was an appointment at a health clinic for a thorough check up. I knew that this clinic served senior executives of large companies exclusively and charged appropriately high fees. I was flattered to think of the trouble Evelyn must have gone through to get me the appointment. As a bonus, I may at last get a chance to mix with the mighty; who knows, the CEO of Very Large Oil Corporation may be in the reception room at the same time and may even glance at me as he looked up from the file he was working on. I did not ask whether the fee was part of the birthday gift or not.

I received instructions by fax, cloaked as request, from the clinic to go to a special medical lab at a certain hour two days before the appointment. Lo and behold! there was no throng of sick and dying people in the reception area. A charming lab tech got the details of my age, health history, drug, alcohol and tobacco consumption and took me to a cubicle furnished with a comfy chair and a number of current journals. She asked me to bare my arms. I said I did not carry any. She laughed at the joke and advised me to take off my jacket and shirt but no more. She returned just as I had hung the shirt on the hook at the back of the door. She took out a syringe and other paraphernalia from a shelf and rubbed alcohol on my arm which I was not allowed to lick. Then she proceeded to extract syringe after syringe of blood till I felt wobbly. She must have noticed it, because she stopped, put a band-aid on my arm and left asking me to dress up and wait for the next technician.

I will make the long story short. I was taken to various cubicles for X-Rays, ECG and various scans I had never heard of. I had to undress my upper half in each cubicle and dress again at the end of the test. The tests the clinic had ordered took longer than all the tests performed on my admittedly aging body in its fifty years. Just as well that I lost the count of tests performed on me and did not guesstimate the charges to be included in clinic's fees. Thank goodness it was only once in fifty years. I did not expect to be around fifty years hence, whatever the results of the test.

I entered the hallowed reception hall of the clinic at the appointed minute. Alas! No CEO, CFO, or even COO was waiting there. As soon as I uttered my name, I was led into the office of Dr. Telltale. The venerable doctor was sitting on a large rubber ball absorbed in looking at some charts. He looked up after a minute or two, motioned me to sit down and continued his study of the charts in the file uttering exclamations of surprise every now and then. When he had examined the last chart, he closed the file and looked me over from head to waist. The rest of me was hidden from him behind the desk. After completing his visual examination of me, he decided to end my suspense. He told me that some of the test results were adequate but many had flashed warning signs. He had decided on a series of actual physical endurance tests for me before he could judge the state of my health. He hoped that I had kept the day free because the tests would take up the rest of the day.

I called my office to cancel my appointments and the doctor handed me over to a suitably white coated female assistant, Dr. Shipshape. Dr. Shipshape directed me to the male washroom and suggested I change into appropriate attire for a workout. Garments I may need were on the counter in the washroom and there was a locker for my clothes. I changed into shorts and tee-shirt, found right-sized sneakers and met Dr. Shipshape near the water cooler. She asked me whether I needed a drink. I declined and we were off to the races. Yes, races, on a treadmill. She set the speed very low at first and then increased it steadily till I was running as if I were being chased by a female dragon. Just when I was about to collapse with exhaustion, the machine stopped after a measured slowdown. Dr. Shipshape pressed a button and the treadmill spewed out a long graph. Something was obviously out of shape, judging from the grim countenance of the doctor.

The exercycle, stair-master, push ups, sit ups, lifting of different weights in increments of 1 kilogram and exercises I hadn't heard of followed. Thankfully, I was allowed to recover my breath for precisely 302 seconds after each set of exercises. The reaction of the doctor made it clear that my performance was below that of her other patients. I now knew why I had not risen to the high levels attained by her clientele in the business world. I did not have he physical capacity to perform high endurance feats. Without physical endurance, mental abilities are suspect in the new millennium.

When all the tests were done and I had reached the end of my endurance, Dr. Shipshape asked, nay requested, me to return after a week for a final review with Dr. Telltale. She did tell me that normally this review takes less than fifteen minutes but I should allow an hour. Obviously, there was a lot wrong with me that needed correction. When I revealed my fears to my wife, she nodded agreement as if to say she knew this all along and tests were a way to convince me that all was not well in the physique of this dumbbell.

Dr. Telltale was to the point as suits a busy doctor, "Your weight is consistent with the height of six feet but you are only five feet two inches tall. Since you cannot do much to increase your height, in fact it will start to shrink soon, you will have to lose weight. I strongly recommend discipline rather than enrolling in any of the popular weight loss programs. Get off alcohol and cigarettes – not even a celebratory champagne glass or cigar. Cut out desserts, and eliminate, at least for a while, fried foods from your diet." After the lecture, he prescribed an exercise regimen of an hour a day, seven days a week to get my heart and lungs back in shape and my muscle tone to what it should be. His final clincher was the observation that my physical age was sixty five but if I followed his advice to the letter, it could be sixty in a year and fifty five by the time I was that age. Then, I could look forward to a long life as long as I stuck to the prescribed regimen of exercise and restricted diet. Whether I would want to live long under those conditions was not the doctor's consideration. Dr. Shipshape explained a set of exercises to be done twice every day. They were different than back and knee exercises I was doing already and had to be added on. Dr. Telltale said that his report would be sent by e-mail to their client, my wife, within the next half hour.

My dearest doctor had read the report by the time I got home. She had already adjusted the alarm clock for 4:00 AM and I was to start the evening routine at eight. No stone was to be left unturned to make me live long. I will have to; I have no time now to write down for posterity what is in my head.

5

A few months ago, Evelyn asked me to stop by at local grocery store on my way home and pick up some milk. I carefully tied a red string on my right wrist to remind me of her request. The string bracelet did do its job all day whenever I pulled up my sleeve. But my luck ran out yet again. Just as I approached the shopping plaza on my way home, the radio started playing my favourite Mozart tune – Twinkle, twinkle, little star. I joyfully hummed the tune watching the back of the shiny red sports car ahead. I was still humming when I got home. "Where is the milk?" my wife asked. "Oh God, I forgot," I exclaimed and rushed back to the store.

A week later I got a call from my family doctor. She was

very friendly. For a while I wondered if she was inviting me for a rendezvous. No such luck. She was reminding me that I was due for a check up and she had a cancellation that afternoon. If I missed the opportunity, I may have to wait longer than I should at my age. In my state of health, I could not turn down such an urgent invitation made in so sweet a manner. A few hours later, I was reading an old Time magazine in the examination room, dressed only in my underwear. Just when I was in the middle of an interesting essay on mental illness, the doctor walked in.

She did her usual thing, pronounced me physically fit and asked me to dress up and come down to her office. I became rather nervous. Was I going to be fired because I was not making enough visits to justify being on her patient list? Had she seen my letters in the paper complaining about Drug Company-sponsored golf trips? Was there something wrong with me that couldn't be told in my state of undress?

I hurriedly dressed up and knocked timidly on her office door. She asked me to come in and sit down across the desk from her. She said she was too busy to beat around the bush and came straight to the point. The point was that I was acting forgetful and there was a possibility she wanted to rule out. The possibility was that I was in early stages of Alzheimer's disease. If I was agreeable, she would set up an appointment with the Alzheimer's ward in the local research hospital for necessary tests. This came as a relief after all my earlier fears. I readily agreed. Her office called the following week and I presented myself in good time at the reputed clinic.

I was introduced to a nationally renowned psychologist and his pretty young assistant. The Freud look alike explained to me in German-accented English that they needed to check how various compartments of my brain functioned. To do this, they had a standard test developed after decades of research in a variety of environments. His assistant would conduct the test. I was to follow her in a sound proof cubicle a few doors away. The lady directed me to the washroom so I could be fully relaxed before the exhausting exercise. When I entered the room, she told me that I could stop for a break whenever I felt tired. There was water on the table and coffee down the hall. A muffin could be arranged whenever I wished. I thanked her and took a gulp of water. She handed me a pencil and a writing pad and my journey to Psychville began.

After a couple of hours of drawing various items from memory, repeating letters and numbers in forward and reverse order, explaining the meaning of words I had rarely heard of, doing complicated arithmetic operations like two and three digit additions without the calculator, identifying crude line sketches of animals and inanimate objects, playing something similar to tic-tac-toe, I was told that I was done for now. She would let me know soon if more tests were needed. Otherwise, the report would be on my doctor's desk in a week.

Much to my disappointment, I never heard from the assistant. I did hear from the doctor though. She told me that there was not much to worry since the disease was not sufficiently advanced yet. However, the front lobe of my brain was in worse state than the rest. It meant that my faculty for judgment was suspect. Therefore, I should avoid making critical decisions on my own till she had arranged for a neurologist to check me out. Again, I readily agreed.

When I got home and told this to my wife, expecting some sympathy. She said she was not at all surprised. She reminded me all the occasions when I had disagreed with her as examples of my failing judgment. I did not get the kind words I was hoping for but I was now relieved of the responsibility of making critical decisions like what colour should the bedroom be painted in, whether to shovel the snow or leave it for a later day, when the clothes needed dry cleaning – you know what I mean. But I still had to paint the bedroom in colours specified by her, shovel snow when told to, and take clothes to drycleaners every Friday. My driving was now suspect and I took public transport to work. My main occupation is the investment of my family's savings. In the new regimen, I had to contact my wife or daughters when I wanted to do a stock trade, explain to them what and why in full detail and wait for their concurrence. They usually asked me to wait till they had checked behind my back with the broker. Fortunately, the broker always supported the trades; after all he made his living from trading commissions. However, the prices changed during this exercise and it often became too late to profit from the trade. This restriction brought the growth of the last few years in the investment portfolio to a sudden halt, but it was considered worthwhile in order to protect the savings from evaporating due to bad judgment of an old man with the rotting frontal lobe.

There were other changes in my life too. I was discouraged from joining in social events. Grandchildren were not left with me alone unless they were asleep. My opinions were not sought and, if offered, were coolly disregarded. When I look back, this was always the way in our matriarchal family. Am I becoming overly sensitive? Sensitivity is not known to be a frontal lobe activity. I better keep this observation to myself. I would not like my family to be concerned for my welfare in the few spare moments of their busy lives.

# My Writing Career

## 1

I am a man with a short fuse. It takes very little to get me upset. When it is a relationship matter, I shower curses on the culprit. When it is a media story or comment, I fire a letter off to the Editor. For a long time the media paid even less attention to my missiles than my friends did. They never responded in person nor published any of my letters. It did not discourage me however. The letters were the means of letting off steam. They served the purpose wonderfully with no offence to anybody.

One fine morning the whole scene changed. It was a long weekend, a holiday weekend. There were only a few letters in the Editor's mailbox and he had to scramble among the previous day's rejects to fill the space. One of these lucky letters was mine, complaining about fat squirrels in my yard scaring my cat from going outdoors on a fine day. I was amazed the next morning to see my name in print for the first time since I was arrested in a case of mistaken identity by the crime squad ten years or more ago. But this was nothing compared to what happened two days later. There, on the *Letters to the Editor* page was my name again. A squirrel lover had taken me to task for hating hard-working, joyful, freedom-loving squirrels and preferring lazy worthless pets like cats. I was amused that some one could love such wasteful and noisy creatures and hate beautiful slim and slender cats. But my amusement was utterly overshadowed by the thrill of seeing my name in the media twice in three days. It had never happened before and I thought it would never happen again.

My dear reader, I was wrong again. There must have been a drastic change in the editorial policies in national and regional newspapers and magazines. It may have been e-mail mania that got hold of me. Since my typing was awfully slow, the letters became short and pointed. I skipped on detailed reasoning but always included an amusing line. Editors liked the short letters with a touch of humour. They started publishing my fulminations. Before I knew it, my name was everywhere; once a week in the national paper, twice a week locally, in every other issue of the popular weekly magazine. I was thrilled to bits. Friends from far and wide read my letters and called to congratulate me. Proud as punch, I e-mailed them to my daughters scattered over the continent.

"Mom, Daddy's letters are full of *non-sequiturs,* how do they get published?" My wife Evelyn showed me the e-mail from a professor in Pennsylvania. I should have anticipated this kind of ego-puncturing response from an egghead; after all she was my daughter. Just to be sure, I looked in the dictionary for the meaning of *non-sequitur.* Then I looked critically at a few of the published letters to see what inference did not follow from previous statements. I had to agree that there was some truth in her statement. However, I did feel that a letter must be brief to have any chance of publication and there is little room to develop an argument. I e-mailed her this rather lame excuse for *non-sequiturs.* She promptly proved me wrong by publishing in our respected national newspaper a well-argued five hundred word letter. She rubbed my nose further in the dirt by another small letter which was duly academic in tone and content. As if not to be left behind, Evelyn and our youngest daughter did the same.

Somewhat discouraged, I gave up and did not write for a few weeks. Then, something got my goat and a few incoherent lines hit the screen of the Letter Editor of the national newspaper. There must have been a shortage of correspondents and the letter, after extensive editing, adorned the bottom of the last *Letters* column in the paper the next day. This encouragement opened the floodgates of my creativity and added considerably to the workload of Canada's leading newspapers and magazines. Even *Time* magazine did not escape my onslaught. There were letters on business and finance, national affairs, international affairs, arts and social affairs. Sports escaped my wrath because Canadian papers avoid cricket and soccer. Copies of letters commenting on columnists were duly sent to them, although, judging from the response, these met the fate of other unsolicited mail. One day last November I reached the peak of stardom in the Letters-to-the-Editor firmament. Four different letters were published in four different journals that Monday. From this point on, there was nowhere to go but down. So I decided to retire. No more letters pestered Letter Editors for a while.

Something trivial, like our revered leader adorning the front pages of all our newspapers every day of the week, caught my eye. The creative juices flowed again and my letters lampooning the legacy of the great man hit the *Letters* column. Then an unfortunate event happened. A young overseas student fatally neglected her babies after she was left stranded by their father who happened to be a local drug dealer. Newspapers made much of her callousness. On the other hand, the father was never mentioned. It struck me that he shared the blame equally by disappearing when fathers are needed the most. I wrote to two Editors pointing this out. Unfortunately, my well-constructed letters were consigned to the 'delete' button by both. I complained to them pointing out the importance of the subject. The editors came down from their respective pedestals and told me that they had to give letters from other correspondents a chance and, if I wrote fewer letters, my best letters would have a better chance of being accepted.

This made me think - now I will write only when something really irked me. However, being an irksome fellow, something is always bothering me. And being opinionated to boot, I have this irrepressible urge to tell every one what I think. Vainglorious, Marcus Aurelius called my type in his *Meditations*. Around this time a respected Canadian weekly published a long article on physical fitness. It prompted me to write a carefully crafted letter describing how the mania for fitness had saved my life when I got separated from my party in a forest and spent three days walking in rain without any food before making my way out. The editor liked the letter and published it, but without the experience in the forest. I complained about dropping the lines that prompted the letter in the first place. The letter editor afforded me the courtesy of a reply – that was all the space he had.

A rebuff like this would have made any sensible person quit. After all the writer of a published letter doesn't get paid, it takes a while to write and, judging from recent silence of friends, nobody reads the letters any more, at least mine. It is discouraging to an egotist like me to take all that trouble and not be acknowledged as the master of an almost forgotten art. Worst of all, if a submitted letter is rejected one loses interest in the rest of the journal. This in itself may not be bad considering all the depressing news of late. Yet, as every ex-smoker knows, it is hard to give up a bad habit. Back I went to reading the depressing news, picking the most annoying one and responding to it with a letter. Letters did not take long to write. But editors like a punch line even if it is a *non-sequitur*. It was thinking a punch line with appropriate humour that took time. And time was in short supply. Not because I was as busy as most of my retired friends seemed to be - I was not retired. All this had to be done when the boss was not looking. And it had to be done in time for it to reach the Editor before he finalized his selection. The pressure was immense, but instead of slowing me down, it spurred me on.

2

My entry appeared in the Ethics column of the *Globe and Mail* this morning. I was surprised because it was done in a rush and not up to my usual standard. Quite possibly, some agency pulled out an ad at the last minute, leaving a hole just the size of my contribution. I know that not many people look at the Careers section and even fewer are interested in Ethics. Yet, it boosted my ego to see my name in print. Then I did something which I had never done before. The website of the newspaper has recently added an archive feature. One can search any item from the files of the national newspaper of Canada going back to 2002. I punched my name in the appointed space and typed go. To my utter surprise, that morning's entry was the 99th time I had appeared in the paper.

Now, there is nothing special about the number 99, the Great One Gretzky excepted. But this made me think. Should I stop at the peak of two digits and retire at the top or make a go for the bottom of three digits. Being a centurion does have some merit. I couldn't honestly say that the *Globe* has published hundreds of my submissions now. It will only be a slight exaggeration after one more acceptance. O.K., the decision is made. I am making a go for the century.

Easier said than done. By hook or by crook, I have sneaked into many different columns over the last four years. Which column should be bestowed the honour of my landmark entry? It can't be a Letter to the Editor. They published one only the other day and the filter on the Editor's computer will remove my letters for the next month or two. I haven't appeared in *Morning Smile* for a while. However, my last joke failed to elicit a smile from family members ranging in age from one to sixty even when I told it for the tenth time. No, Mr. Dithers having fewer waffles at breakfast won't do. And I am too tense to think of a new pun. One has to be relaxed for his decaying frontal lobe to spew out a one-liner suitable for the bottom right hand corner of page 2 of the glorious *Globe*.

What else can I come up with? I can't arrange an interview with a correspondent. My only interview was a long time ago when a neophyte correspondent called me in error. The interview did make the front page even though the half-hour session was edited to a mere half-sentence. In an attempt to break into voice media, I have been wining and dining a CBC interviewer for quite a while. She is aware of my wide ranging accomplishments but hasn't even considered me once. Why would a complete stranger interview someone out of the blue?

I have made occasional appearances on 'Challenge' in the *Book Section* on Saturdays. I spend the whole weekend scratching my bald head attempting to come up with three funny answers to the problem set every week. I e-mail my answers first thing on Monday to free my brain to attend to my job. The Editor, however, does not appreciate my sense of humour. He consigns my entries to the 'delete' bin and then empties the bin to make sure they get no second chance. An odd entry escapes this fate once in a while, appears in print and shocks me into spilling my morning tea in bed. In spite of having to change sheets, perhaps because of it, I feel more proud than I do when my daughter wins medals in her international races. However, the chances of another entry making it are small. The Editor is in a foul mood because his favourite entrant has switched to the *National Post* and he can't bear the sight of entries from also-rans like me. What other reason is there for my entries biting the dust for so long? I have to face it; chances of a 100th appearance being on 'Challenge' are remote.

The *Report on Business* magazine section has welcomed my letters a couple of times. But ads have now replaced the Letters page. That leaves the trusty old Ethics column. But I just got published this morning. There may not be many readers of this column but there are a lot of contributors. This particular editor has taken her cue from the Letters editor. For all I know, the two distinguished arbiters of contributors' fate may be the same person. She wants to give every contributor a chance. That deprives the readers from my great entries for weeks, sometimes months. There is no chance the Editor will give up this unfair practice and include an entry from me soon, even if I put my best foot forward.

No, I must wait for a decent interval of few weeks to pass before I can hit the century. No problem, patience is the English equivalent of my name. However, with my luck, the website will extend the library back by another year by then. This will add my earlier entries to the current 99 and all this fretting will be for naught. I will be a centurion but miss out the joy of accomplishment from the hundredth hit. Well, that is life. I take what the gods, and Editors, give me.

3

I must have got up on the right side of the bed, or my wife's smile when I served her tea in bed was special, it may even have been my new suit. Although it was raining on this cool late May morning, I was feeling great and hummed my favourite Mahler melody all the way to my consulting business. A message was waiting there for me. Call 1-800-rush-now as soon as possible. In my rush to call, I knocked the coffee cup on to my suit. I was cursing on top of my voice when I heard 'hello' on the ear piece. I apologized profusely to the speaker. He responded that he got similar responses quite often. "Must be selling something useless," I thought. Wrong again. It was the assistant editor of our illustrious national newspaper. "We are setting up a citizens' forum on our website. Each member will contribute a 500 word article once a week during the election campaign. You have been highly recommended by our Letters section. Will you be able to do that for us?"

"Well, I did not expect such an honour. I am flattered."

"Great, much obliged. Will you be able to send your picture and a short biography by e-mail?"

"I can't send my picture by e-mail. I can mail it to you."

"Sorry, that will take too long. Can you courier that to me?"

"Sure, my fee will cover the cost, I suppose."

"I apologise sir, my mistake. It is not customary to pay web columnists. You don't mind, do you?"

"I don't mind, but I am disappointed. I hope my disappointment is not reflected in my picture, or worse in my columns."

"Don't worry, sir. We will edit it out, if necessary."

Leaving my work behind, I rushed home via a passport photo booth, scribbled a tall tale called *Bio* and sent it and the picture by Alwayslater. Oh yes. I also changed into a coffee coloured suit and dropped the stained suit at the drycleaners. By the time I got back to the office, clients were screaming because their calls were not returned promptly. I told them that they are dealing with a national columnist and some patience will be in order for the next few weeks. Their rather cool response gave me a sinking feeling that being patient will be my lot if I want to be in the consulting business for long.

My bio and picture appeared after some editing. The Editor's attempt to make me look intelligent and influential misfired and my colleagues did not even try not to snigger. I consoled myself that it couldn't matter very much; not many readers, indeed if there are any, were likely to know me personally. Alas! Woe is me. Just as I was putting the brimming coffee cup down, the phone rang. My rush to get the phone caused the inevitable spill, this time on a map it had taken hours to prepare. It was my major client laughing himself silly, if a client can ever be silly. He had seen the picture and couldn't resist telling me how much the picture looked like me when I am trying to look important. I thanked him and hoped secretly that he wouldn't be making such sarcastic remarks after my columns. The jobs of fifteen people depended on his good graces.

Election Date was announced and the editor e-mailed asking for my first column that evening. I cancelled a staff meeting in the afternoon and wrote my 500 words. I showed it to my personal editor, my wife. She said it was good but needed some work to clarify some thoughts. I cancelled my bridge game and reworked the words till they matched the thoughts - hers. I had to be careful. There was a reader out there who held the destiny of my consulting career in his hands. It was nearly midnight when my dear and patient (doctor actually) wife approved my write up. I pressed the send button and went directly to bed too exhausted to brush my teeth.

Election campaign went on and on, and a lot of hot air, enough to cause global warming on its own, was blown through TV and the print media into already hot homes during the blistering summer month. I kept my cool and submitted my columns, after the due stamp of approval, and they were published without much editing. I breathed a sigh of relief after submitting my last 499 words before the election and took my only known reader to lunch at his favourite restaurant, the most expensive in town. It was worth it. He expressed satisfaction with the opinions I had expounded, even if his convictions were directly opposite. This should have rung an alarm bell, but it didn't. A columnist has to be focused.

I got to the office a little tipsy, having tried to match my client's liquor intake. The secretary gave me an urgent message – the editor wants to get hold of me as soon as I am back. He couldn't want me to rewrite the column; I was in no state to do it. I called him and told him so in no uncertain terms even before he had said hello. He did not interrupt me and when I finished he apologized for leaving a wrong impression in his message. My column was good. So good, in fact, that he wanted me to write one more column, this one after the election results were declared. I was to send my impression of the election within an hour or two of the speeches by the leaders. What can an aspiring columnist do but agree. I assumed that my wife would be watching the results with me and she would not mind staying up a little longer for the sake of her husband's new profession.

Election Day arrived. I survived a hard day in the office and on my way home voted, after much stewing, according to my recommendation in the last column. After a rather rushed dinner of beans on toast, my wife and I sat down with a fresh bottle of scotch and a tumbler of ice to watch the results as they came in. They came in dribs and drabs at first, and then flooded in. At ten the parties were tied with only British Columbia to go. With suspense at its highest point the wretched phone rang. No, it was not the editor. The hospital was calling my wife; a mother was ready to bring a new baby into the world to work hard all its life to pay our pension. The call pulled the rug from under my feet. "But, but, but I need you to approve my column," I blabbered. No luck. She rushed out saying, "You can do it."

At last, almost all the results were out. The wrong party won. Speeches went on till one minute before midnight. After slurping the last drop from the bottle, I started writing. I wrote what I could in my foul mood and drunken stupor. Looking back, the write up was bad, even for me. I cursed the media, particularly the publisher of the national paper for taking sides, thereby ensuring that the corrupt and incompetent party had won. After filling my quota of five hundred words in this vein, I waited for my wife to approve it - in vain. She called to say there were complications; she didn't know when she would be back. Frustrated, I pressed the 'send' button. As soon as I had done it I wished I had pressed the 'delete' button.

The editor called in the morning as I put the phone down after a lecture on media writing by my only known reader. "I can't publish this vituperative outpouring. You are insulting my boss and my paper. This is the best paper to work for. I can't afford to be fired." On and on he went. I butted in when he stopped for air, "Look, you wanted my opinion on elections, you have it. To publish it or not is your decision. Edit it the way you like. I did my job, now you do yours." He took me on my word, took all the negatives out and published it. The published version did credit to the editor as much as to me. It was something I would have really written if I were sober when writing it.

Writing these columns was so much fun. Needless to say I am waiting with bated breath for another call from the editor.

4

After my month in the glare of web I returned to my humble calling with renewed vigour. Colleagues and family egged me on. The shower of letters became a torrent. Editors were inundated. They screamed for help. No help was forthcoming. So they did the only thing they could. They asked me, courteously at first, firmly later, to send fewer letters. Some said once a week, others once a month. When entreaties failed, they installed filters on their computers to automatically delete my letters for a specified number of days after one of my letters was published. The stream of published letters became a trickle. A flabbergasted friend called asking why he hadn't seen my letters for a while. To have my opinion find voice on so few world shattering events was intolerable now that I had become used to my voice getting a wide coverage. Something had to be done.

Lo and behold! Another great letter writer stepped onto the planet. Swami Ananda was born fully mature out of the head of a frustrated writer. He went to work the day of his birth. Editors started receiving letters from a garrulous gentleman with my office address and phone number as his home. The letters were short and to the point. They were irate but also had a humorous line in them. Editors published them without any suspicion about their origin. In one year, I published one hundred letters and the Swami ninety. No one knew that Swami was really me but this anonymity didn't bother me in the least. My views were getting the airing they deserved and that is what gave me the pleasure now. What difference did it make whether my name appeared a hundred times or two hundred times? Who was counting; except me of course.

It is a sad fact of life that every good thing comes to an end. Those who are born must die. A letter from Swami mentioned some statistic which the Editor wanted to check. He called the phone number and got my message. Of course he was furious. He left a message saying that this trickery had to stop unless I wanted to be blacklisted from the whole newspaper chain. To say that the message disturbed me is the understatement of the decade. But the knife had another stab left. The phone rang again. The editor of the ocal paper had noticed that letters from Swami Ananda were from my e-mail header. He wanted to know why? I made some lame excuse but knew that the eitor was not fooled.

A proud author can absorb one strike. But two in such quick succession are deadly. I decided that Swami's time had come and gone. It was time to lay him to rest; provide him a suitable burial. I wrote a death notice for the local and national papers announcing the passing of my friend who had left no immediate survivors and whose major achievement was over a hundred published letters in reputable papers. I was quite happy to pay for the notices although very sorry that a noble voice had been stilled by editors reading too much Sherlock Holmes.

Swami's death was not in vain. It had the potential to change the course of literature. In the short term, it reduced the work load of *Letter* editors. In the long term, I now lost interest in writing letters and had the irresistible urge to grow out of 100 word pieces into larger works. To help me along, my wife booked me on a ten-week course in Creative Writing in the local community college. The course was given by a well-known author who had published a popular novel and several stories and essays. I was nervous about attending it but the good wife wisely suggested that attending classes after a hiatus of thirty years might teach me some discipline, if nothing else.

I rushed through dinner on the evening of the first lecture and drove to my class in good time to make sure of convenient parking and a front seat. When I got to the parking lot reserved for visitors and pretend-students like myself, I realized that I should have left much earlier. The lot was full and several cars were parked along the road. Being an obedient follower that I am, I parked my car in this line up and walked to my lecture hall with some trepidation. All seats in the front and back rows were already taken. So I took a second row seat behind a couple of older ladies almost as short as myself.

Events unfolded to prove that my nervousness was well-founded. At seven sharp, the teacher entered the room with the dignified carriage of a published author. Remembering my days as a student in times long gone by I stood up in her honour. However, no one else in the class did so. Sheepishly, I sat down and stared at the blank pages of my note book wondering why the students chose not to show any respect to the teacher. The workman like teacher was not perturbed by this and asked us to introduce ourselves to the rest of the class in a few words.

"My name is David Chu. I teach Chinese literature at the

college. I am here to learn how writing in English is different than in Mandarin."

"My name is Kamala Varuchandran. I teach Malaysian dance. I am here to learn how I can write about my unusual experiences."

"I am Fernando Porcile. I give private Portuguese lessons. I think I need to learn some basics of writing in English so I can translate Portuguese classics into English."

After these exotic introductions, I wondered if I was in an "English for old Immigrants" class or a preliminary grouping for a human zoo. It was soon my turn to contribute. "I am Sudhir Jain. I work as a consultant. I want to learn how to tell funny stories so my clients do not notice my bad advice," I blurted out. Every one burst out laughing, much to my chagrin. I wished the floor would open and land me with a thud on the desks in the lecture hall on the lower floor. But like most of my wishes, this too went unfulfilled.

The introductions carried on in this vein. I was too mortified to pay any attention. My stupor was interrupted by a tap on my shoulder. I looked up to the teacher who was looking at me with amusement. "Let us all wake up, if we want to be forgiven our follies," she said to much laughter and my embarrassment. She picked up a thick book, showed it to us and (wo)mandated that we obtain a copy. This was to be the text for the course and we were expected to read a chapter in preparation for each lesson. I wondered how I will manage that. It was a long time ago when I read a full page before falling asleep, even of a James Bond novel.

The rest of the lesson was a continuous harping on one theme – write every day for half an hour, doesn't matter what and doesn't matter when." Looking at me she added, "Even if it is in between meeting clients seeking your advice." It added to my mortification and I wondered if I had ever met her at some party and been less than respectful. Not very likely, though, she was an attractive woman. She finished the lesson by suggesting that we bring our "works" for reading aloud in the class. I thought of my unique accent and my illegible writing and wondered how I would manage. Well, my family is sure to have suggestions; they are the ones who got me in this hot lemon pickle.

An unpleasant surprise waited for me at the car. It was a yellow slip informing me that I owed the city $101.29 for unlawful parking. No other car had the slip on its window. "Victimised again, and it isn't even Friday the thirteenth," I thought. Every driver knows how futile it is to protest the traffic fines. You save a lot of time and bother by just paying it and taking it out of the kid's allowance in small fines for real or phony transgressions. It keeps them straight too.

When I got home every one wanted to know what I had learnt. Rather than disappoint them with an honest answer, I asked their advice on how I could handle reading to the class what I am supposed to write when waiting for the clients?

"No problem, Dad. Just speak slowly, as you would approach a green light when you are thinking of an excuse for being late," said my teenage daughter.

"Good idea" Her mother agreed and added with a wink, "but it will take some work."

"I will show them," I thought to myself. "I cannot change my accent but I can slow down, just by timing my words to my thinking, rather than speaking thoughtlessly like a Greyhound bus approaching an orange light."

So I spent my time between clients writing about nothing in particular and practicing slow speech. My colleagues wondered what was going on. When I told one of them what I was doing and why, the word spread like wildfire. They all swore never to write a letter to the editor whatever the provocation. I don't expect editors ever to thank me for the work I am saving them. I never get credit that is due to me. My good deeds are performed without fanfare.

The week passed quickly. In the next lesson, one wannabe poet read a heart-rending poem about the spouse who contacted

AIDS, a budding novelist read the introduction to his ground-breaking novel about Israel before the birth of Christ, a young woman read a short story about love without sex. According to the rules of common courtesy, all comments were 'supportive' and not one helpful suggestion passed any lips. This encouraged me to read my essay - very slowly - on how to get the best out of a cabbie; don't expect him to help with your cases, don't bang the door shut, don't tap him on the shoulder, be friendly but not intimate and for heaven's sake don't ask him how long he has been in Canada or why he is driving a cab in Canada and not practicing medicine in his home country. A silence greeted my presentation. After a small pause, the teacher said that it was a good effort but she would like to read it before making any comments. Obviously, slow did not mean comprehensible.

By the time the last lesson arrived, fellow class-mates had become somewhat familiar with my accent. In my latest piece I extolled the virtues of life in Canada and anticipated the joys of life here for my daughters, without them having to date the locals and find their own mates. I got a standing ovation. The teacher encouraged me to keep writing and suggested journals where I could submit this essay for publication. I followed her advice, albeit with some trepidation.


6


I got to the office at 7:59:35 following Monday and opened my e-mail. After eight junk mails which were deleted unread, there was one from an Editor of *Around the World*. I opened the mail with great anticipation. "I like the essay, I want to publish it, do not send it anywhere else, send an invoice for $12.50, sorry cannot promise the date of publication, will inform one day in advance if possible."

My joy knew no bounds. Now I could claim to be a published author. Any Tom, Dick or Jane can claim to be an author but only a few can claim to be published. I was one of those few thousands. I had got there by hard work and was the living proof that lack of talent can be overcome if one tried hard enough. I told every one whether they wanted to listen or not and sent them the essay on the slightest provocation without ever wondering why no one responded with any comment.

I started getting up early so I could walk down to the newsstand for the paper with my essay. I checked my e-mail every few minutes risking being fired from the job I loved. Sorry, no luck. A week went by, then a month. My wife suggested a week with the grandchildren in the Boondocks where they don't know if there is a Canada, leave alone Canadian newspapers. Wife's word is supreme as it should be when one is married to such a superlative woman. We packed and left for Boondocks one Friday morning after checking *Around the World*, of course. We had a wonderful time looking after the tiny tots when their parents took time off for their own rest and recreation.

We got back home late Sunday after next. I got back into the routine of getting up early to check the paper on Monday. No luck. I entered the office in a despondent mood and opened the electronic mail box. Shining brightly among scores of junk and not so junk messages was one from the Editor – "I am glad to inform you that your essay will appear on Thursday. The check will follow." That was the preceding Thursday, one of the days when I was basking in the glory of being a grandfather. How do I get the old newspaper?

I was naturally restless at work. At last the lunch hour arrived. I drove to the store downtown that sells the newspapers from around the world. I asked for the last Thursday's edition of our self-proclaimed national newspaper *Around the World*. "We don't keep papers older than three days," said the man on the counter looking at me as if I was asking for the moon. I apologized profusely for interrupting his game of solitaire. On the way back to work I called Travis Boulder on my cell. Travis is a subscriber of the newspaper and gets up at six sharp to read it cover to cover. "Sorry, recycled the papers over the weekend. Why do you want it?" Travis asked. "Will tell you later," I said switching off the phone.

Once again, the answer was staring me in the face – the main city library. They keep old papers and loan one to you just for the asking. They don't even check your library card before handing the requested newspaper. Sneaking out with a page of it when they are busy with the lunch hour crowd should not be difficult. I turned the car around, found a meter, pushed plenty of coins in the slot and walked to the newspaper section of the library assuming the air of a man with no care in the world. Under four layers of clothing my heart was beating like crazy, not being accustomed to the sneaking routine. The clerk brought the paper; I took it to a table in a corner and, with my back to the counter, opened the section where the essay usually appears. My mouth fell open.

The essay page had been torn off by some despicable sneak.


## 7


The success encouraged me, but it was to remain the only success. I continued to write essays and short stories of 500 – 3000 words. These were based on experiences in my daily life. Sometimes they were humorous, other times serious. But they all had one thing in common. No editor wanted to publish them. In desperation, I wrote humble letters requesting special consideration to the newspaper which published my short works so often that I felt it depended on me. When humility did not work, I changed my tone and wrote a letter implying that I would stop submitting my short pieces. Not only did the editor refuse to publish the essays, she informed me that there was no shortage of contributors who needed much less editing than my work did. It was a hard pill to swallow, but I had no choice. How to publish the now mounting collection was becoming a major occupation. Then the light flashed when I least expected it.

Movieah is the most popular TV host in the world. She champions literacy, encourages budding artists and authors, and she even has a Book of the Week Club. It struck me that she would surely be impressed by the self-deprecating humour of stories and the poignancy of my essays. She is based in Lotobabe in the state of Healthythen. The Aria Opera there would soon be performing the set of operas I travel long distances to see every year. Why not kill two birds with one stone; go to the operas and show my essays to Movieah in one visit. It shouldn't be too hard to locate her and to read her a few selections.

No sooner thought than done. I secured the last seat for the performances. Then I prepared a neat folder with a green silk covering. I printed my fifty best essays double spaced in easy to read letter size on the finest paper with pages neatly numbered at the bottom right corner. I prepared the index carefully and printed it in an attractive font. The first item on the index was a dedication. The book was dedicated to the most important promoter of Art in the world – Movieah Minfrey – in a flowery language which would have made an author of the Romantic period proud. I adjusted the holes in my three-hole punch with great care and checked before punching holes for each of the fifty essays. It took several tries but eventually I got the whole set properly lined up in the book. I got a close friend who has mastered the art of Calligraphy to write in her best style - *To a Great Supporter of Art from a humble practitioner*. I carefully pasted the red square sheet with black writing on green silk cover. I carefully wiped the book before placing it gingerly in a cardboard box which had been thoroughly vacuumed, wiped and brushed inside out. I hand carried the box in spite of the risks of having to open it for security. Fortunately, security x-rays approved the box without damaging the book. I took greater care in handling the book from home to the hotel in distant Lotobabe than I used to with my baby daughters and do with my granddaughters. Kids recover fast from slight dents, precious books never do.

It wasn't hard to find Movieah's address. From all accounts, she was in town. I didn't want to risk the box getting wet in the rain. Therefore, I waited impatiently for a bright sunny morning. During this waiting period, I prepared my story of being a writer from the frozen Tundra in the North looking for support from the greatest patron of promising unknown artists. The sunny day arrived two days before I was booked to return home. Ten dollars and ten minutes in a cab took me to Movieah's studio. The studio occupied a whole block in a rundown neighbourhood. In fact, the studio itself had a rundown appearance. The cab dropped me near the tail end of a huge line of boisterous young people. After I had been in line for quite a while without moving much, it transpired that the young people were lining up for admission tickets to the recording session the following week, not to shake hands with the greatest TV star of our times. A security guard who was posted there primarily to keep the line from meandering to the road advised me to go to an entrance on west side of the building. I found the west entrance after going full circle round the block. The kindly young lady heard my story with some patience and much amusement. However, she was not the right person. She suggested the keeper of the south entrance may help.

I walked over and found the door locked. After I had waited a while in the hot sun, a middle aged man rushed in to enter through the door. I put my foot in the door and told him my whole story while he tried to close the door on me. From his unpleasant reaction it was clear even to me that calling on Movieah was not going to be as simple as I had imagined. When I screamed with pain from my crushed foot, the man took pity on me. He told me that Movieah only saw men who were either celebrities or unusually handsome.

Since I was neither, all I could do was to leave my book with the Shipping and Receiving. They would make sure it got to the right assistant to the assistant producer of the show. The department is located on the east side.

I limped over to the east side. By now sweat was pouring out of my skin in buckets and the book was in danger of getting wet. Fortunately, the walk was in the shade of next building and the door was open. I rang the bell on the receiving counter and a brash young man came out of the cave. He asked me what I wanted. I began to repeat the whole story but he rudely interrupted, "I don't have all day, come quickly to the point." By now I was at the end of my tether. I stuttered, "I have a book to deliver to Movieah." The kid threw his hands up, "We don't accept hand deliveries. You will have to mail it or send it by courier. If I take your box, I lose my job. Sorry, I have other things to do." He handed me a card with the address and disappeared in his cave.

There was nothing I could do now except to have a cold drink in a café across the street and head for the post office a block away. I wrote a covering note expressing my great disappointment at not seeing the great Movieah in person, enclosed a twenty dollar bill to cover return postage in the unlikely event of her not loving the book, and carefully packed the dainty box with the precious book in a bigger box. With the help of a kindly mail clerk, the book in a box in a box was on its way to the brash young man in shipping and receiving in Movieah's studio.

That was six months ago. I stayed glued to my phone for several weeks. No word ever. I wondered whether the precious book that was to make me immortal got lost in the mail. My wife, who is amazingly prescient in such matters, thought that the shipment had made the brash young man twenty dollars richer and the book made its way through the garbage disposal system of the great city of Lotobabe.

It was the end of October. A prospective publisher for my short story wanted to know if I was a "published" author. A check on the website of the national newspaper revealed that I had appeared there 12 times in 2002, 24 times in 2003, 36 times in 2004 and 43 times so far this year. No, I have not been interviewed, invited to write columns nor appeared with a heartrending tale on the back page. My contributions have been rather humble, away from the headlines and tucked in corners unseen by even the most ardent reader. The quantity was significant, at least in 2005, even though the quality was modest. My contributions were the occasional space-fillers in *Morning Smile* and *Letters to the Editor* which appear every weekday in the Main section, Workplace Ethics 101 on Wednesdays in *Careers*, and The Challenge on Saturdays in *Books*. Not many readers noticed them. If they did, they found them not worthy of a congratulatory note to the author. I am as unnoticed in a public gathering now as I was before my first contribution appeared. Most celebrities wish such anonymity. This anonymous person craves celebrity, albeit just a little. He gets none.

As it turned out, and I should have known, the publisher was not impressed by the kind of published work and consigned my offering to the return basket. But the odd number gave me the idea that, with two months still to go, it would be an achievement to make 50 appearances in one year. The goal, crazy and meaningless though it may be to every one but me, seemed achievable with ease, considering an average of four appearances a month so far and only seven to go in nine weeks. One acceptance in each of my regular columns in November and even fewer in December would do it. In fact, November turned out to be the lucky month with five appearances. With a whole month to go, I was only two short of my goal. I felt that if I achieved this, some kind of glory would come my way, if only because every one I know will hear of it till they start avoiding me like the plague.

It was now the second Sunday in December. I was starting to get worried. One third of the month was gone without an editor giving me the blessing. Still, two appearances in three weeks should not normally be difficult for a prolific contributor who insists on testing the patience of the editors by his daily submissions in a language he learnt late in life. However, the situation had become complicated and a moral dilemma had cropped up. My wife and the daughter had each taken a leaf from my book. Just that morning, my wife submitted a *Morning Smile* and my daughter sent a Letter. They even had the temerity to ask me to edit them. It would have been unethical for me to send my entries in competition with the loved ones. May not have been unethical, but it would have been tactless all the same. If the editor had preferred my submission, I may not have lived to see 50. Accepted submissions that is, not age. I passed that chronological landmark ages ago.

So *The Challenge* and *Ethics* were the two columns left for me. Lo and behold! No new challenge was set that week. That left just one column for two weeks. Last year, the *Ethics* column did not appear during the week after Christmas. That left only one week of the two. Even if my submission made it in one of them, a statistical improbability, I would be one short. What to do?

There were only two ways I could go. I could submit a letter or a *Smile* under a pseudonym. However, even if the trick fooled the editor, no one would have believed me when I claimed it as my contribution. And if the word got to my wife or the daughter with the rejected submission, there would have been a hell to pay. Let us face it; I would not have been able to boast of the achievement to the family. What use is glory if the family does not share in it?

As it turned out, two successive columns of *Ethics 101* published my submissions, again as the last entry on the page and edited to a couple of somewhat disjointed lines. Still, I made fifty, and who would know how insignificant the entries were? When I mentioned my achievement to my daughter, she asked what my fiftieth publication was. When I showed her the precious cutting she snorted. I knew then that I had to do something better to earn the glory I deserved. I had to go out in splendour, not in the ignominy of a meaningless two-liner.

The lightning struck me on my way to the office, like Saul on his way to Damascus: "My goal should really be fifty two – averaging one for every week of the year. Two more in the remaining ten days should be doable. One letter and one challenge and I will be there. No, I don't need the *Morning Smile*; the editor can take the time off for Christmas as he did last year. Goodbye *Business Ethics*. I need quality now, quantity won't do. Oh yes. I can also try for the story on the *Back Page*. The editor may accept a humorous story if only because that is all there is in the in-box. I can send this tale of my misfortune and keep my fingers crossed. Normally, it takes six weeks before she even looks at it and that is too late to count for this year. Still, miracles do happen in the Christmas season, even to a devout Hindu like me. I will submit the tale and pray five times a day facing east; towards the almighty Editor in Toronto of course."

It was December 30. My prayers did not persuade the Editor to recognize the succinct merits of my story. I did get an acceptance in the re-run of the *Challenge*. Obviously, my entries were not fit for the elite company in the first round but I take what I am given. Moreover, the family enjoyed it and that is what matters the most. But the elusive fifty-second remained, what else, elusive. Now with one day left, a Saturday, there were only two possibilities: a letter to the Editor or the acceptance in the *Challenge*. The *Challenge* was almost impossible. After two thousand submissions in ten years of the existence of the column, not once had the Editor favoured me two weeks in a row. To expect him to change his tune at that critical hour was to expect water from a stone. There was really only one course left - a letter the Editor would find irresistible.

Writing an acceptable letter is not as easy as it seems to those who have never sent one. First you must have the right topic. Not a popular one, the Editor is already inundated by such letters. Not an unpopular one either, who would print something no one wants to read? The letter must be on a topic which is in the back of every mind trying to push its way to the front. The problem was that it was too far back in my mind and I was too ruffled to dig deep enough to find it in the few hours left to me.

At the last moment I decided to write about people feeling poorer when every politician and economist was telling them that they were richer. I added the mandatory punch line to make it humorous. What was the punch line? Sorry, the editor edited it out.

9

The stream of rejection slips from local, national and international editors would have discouraged any ordinary writer but I never considered myself ordinary. I felt that all great writers have had to overcome the obtuseness of editors and there was no reason I should be an exception. I was certain that any one who could write so many acclaimed stories, acclaimed by family members and junior colleagues that is, deserved to be published so that the general public had an opportunity to reduce the tedium in their daily lives by reading these anecdotes of amusing events. I decided that the best way to go was to publish a book of the collection of stories.

With this end in view, I carefully arranged a hundred stories in groups and the groups in a sensible order and paid my secretary a week of overtime to make an accurate index, carefully format the manuscript and print double-spaced a hundred copies. I spent a day writing a suitable letter extolling the merits of my work and my mostly imaginary achievements in other fields and sent it with one copy of the manuscript to just about every publisher of fiction in North America. Of course, I sent the mandatory envelope with enough stamps for return postage for the unlikely possibility of the publisher being not cultured enough to appreciate my sense of humour.

It wasn't long before the thick envelopes started filling the mail box, sometimes with a form rejection slip but usually without any attachment. This precluded keeping a list of responding agencies. By the end of the month, my desk was loaded to the ceiling with the rejected manuscripts. Just to make sure that the publishers were unanimous in their ignorant judgment I counted them. Ninety nine, did I miss one? I counted again, then again. I got my reluctant wife to help. There were only ninety nine. That meant that one was lost in the mail, either to or from a publisher. There was no way to know which one or which way.

My ego deflated, I stored the books in the basement intending to use them for gifts to my clients. My wife barred me from giving them to our friends for some reason she did not disclose. I still continued to write and submit to magazine publishers and entered many competitions which thrive on the optimism of us dreamers willing to part with substantial entry fees in the hope of winning a prize as a prelude to a well deserved fame. But the stars did not align and my fame was limited to a shrinking circle of friends.

Several months rolled by. It was my sixtieth birthday. After a harrowing day spent in futile attempts to persuade a client not to cancel a major contract, the traffic on the way home was snarled up due to a multi-car collision on the expressway. As if this was not enough, my dear wife was upset because the special dinner she had prepared had not turned out as she expected. It tasted wonderful to me. When I said so she exploded, "You have no taste buds. I don't know why I kill myself preparing delicious meals for you." But being a kindly soul that she is, her good mood returned and we settled down on a sofa with our cups of special Darjeeling tea with the day's mail.

The mail had several offers of silver, gold and platinum cards and many requests from charities which were promptly consigned to the recycling bin. There was the usual complement of bills put in the "to pay" folder. Then there was a letter from an unknown source. I reluctantly opened it fully expecting another annoying communication. It was a reply from the publisher who had my long lost, and by now forgotten, hundredth copy.

The letter read:

> "I am sorry for the delay in contacting you. My publishing house is devoted to bring out the works of unpublished authors and we are inundated by unsolicited manuscripts from all over the world. It took us a while to get to your submission. We like the content, the style and especially the humour. We believe there is a market for books like yours. We will be happy to edit, rearrange and publish a selection of your stories if they were still available. We focus our resources on promoting the work. Therefore, we offer only a symbolic payment on a first book, $1 advance and 1c per sold copy. However, we guarantee that the book will be reviewed in many leading publications by sympathetic reviewers. Thus, you will receive your due recognition which will assure well-deserved and substantial returns on your next book."

I gulped and read it again. By now my wife was getting nervous – what could the letter contain that had me so absorbed in it? She asked me brusquely, "Why is the letter worrying you? Is a former girlfriend threatening to sue you again?"

"Oh no, nothing like that. In fact it is a birthday gift, the most wonderful gift I could imagine. I read it aloud to her. She moved over and hugged me, "Oh, what wonderful news. I always knew there are people out there who recognize a good work of art when they see it. Let me call Mama, she is such an admirer of your stories; and the kids. Some of the stories are about them and they will be so thrilled to see themselves in a book. Published by an Arkansas publisher no less." I realized for the first time the distinction in being published by a little known house in Arkansas. I gracefully accept recognition wherever it comes from.

To make the long story short, the publisher picked fifty of my least favourite stories, got a well-known local author to write a long critical appraisal as an introduction and selected complimentary lines from it for the back page. The cover was a scene from the Arctic with the title "Stories from a Frozen Land," The copies of the book were duly sent to all the leading English newspapers and magazines. It was reviewed in the first week of December in *Arkansas Gazette, Inuvik Herald, Portpatrick Reporter* and *Darwin News,* all leading publications in their communities. After some difficulty I located the reviews on the web. They were indeed favourable, as promised by the publisher and undoubtedly generated great interest among the literate readers spread over four countries on three continents.

Confident of my established reputation as a published author, I prepared a new manuscript containing the remaining 50 stories from the original collection and twenty new ones. I was wondering on the best course for publishing my second collection when a royalty cheque for $5.19 arrived accompanied by a letter offering me 1,481 unsold copies for the cost of shipping and advising me that they would not be able to publish my other stories.

Far from being discouraged, I prepared a covering letter including quotes from critics in the distant lands and an offer to go on promotional tours at my own cost. It must have impressed the publishers I sent the letters to. I received a reply from every house I contacted. None was the standard rejection slip. None was an acceptance either.

Sadly, a Somerset Maugham of the new millennium was nipped in the bud by insensitive, short-sighted, greedy-for-obscene profit publishers acting in consort. What a pity.

## 10

*At one stage of my writing career I interviewed prominent members of our community for the monthly broadsheet the community puts out. I interviewed the top business leaders, bigwigs in provincial and national politics, former and future Olympians and budding and famous writers. But the greatest personality I was fortunate enough to meet under this pretext was Swami Dharyananda during my visit to India to attend a family wedding. The following is the transcript of that interview.*

☙❧

In ten years since its rediscovery by Swami Dharyananda (saint who knows the bliss of patience) in a remote ashram on a snow-capped peak, Psychopathy has shaken the traditional medicine world like an earthquake of magnitude 10. It is a proof, if one were needed, of the wide gulf between traditional and modern medicine systems that little is known about Psychopathy or Swami in so-called Ethical Medicine circles. In order to make our readers aware of the most important development in health care for several decades we requested an interview with the Swami at his convenience. After a thorough check of this interviewer's credentials, the chief of staff of the reclusive Swami agreed to let him be interviewed exclusively for publication in this journal. Final script was approved by the Swami himself after many alterations to "improve the accuracy".

Sudhir: The most revered Swami, what set you on this holy path?

Swami: In the holy year of 1978 I received my degree in Naturopathy from Traditional School of Proven Medicine and attended a ceremony to welcome new graduates into the noble profession. In his carefully chosen words of greeting, the Health Minister extolled the virtues of simplicity and humility and ridiculed the greed and vanity so common in the practitioners of modern medicine. He urged new naturopaths to avoid these all-too-common vices and to make service of fellow citizens main goal in their lives. The exhortation touched me to the core of my being. In a trance, I travelled for two days and two nights by train, bus, donkey cart and foot to the ashram of Maharishi Prakashananda (saint who has seen the light). I rubbed the dust from Maharishi's bare right foot on my forehead and waited till his divine eyes settled mesmerizingly on me. I begged Maharishi to be merciful and show me, a humble naturopath, how I could truly serve the humankind. Maharishi pierced me with his penetrating gaze for what seemed like eternity. Satisfied of my mettle, he ordered me to take a vow of abstinence from all pleasures of the flesh including sex. I did so at once without a single thought for the desires of my young and rather demanding wife. Pleased by this sacrifice, Maharishi set me on a rigorous training course which consisted of yoga, chanting of mantras (religious verses) and meditation when I was not cooking, hauling water or doing errands.

Sudhir: The most accomplished healer, how did you receive enlightenment?

Swami: Long hours of meditation and unstinting devotion to the Maharishi had an unforeseen outcome. I developed a unique psychic intuition. This enabled me to diagnose root causes of the ailments of fellow disciples when they were under or over the weather without even a cursory examination. I then used my training in naturopathy to prescribe herbs and salts appropriate for their condition. The combination of psychic intuition and naturopathy worked wonders and had the sick back in meditation the same evening. After a few such cases the Maharishi realised that his tireless devotee had inadvertently rediscovered the ancient healing art of Psychopathy mentioned in ancient scriptures but lost in upheaval during the invasion of Alexander the Great Geek. The approval of tradition enhanced my thrill as Maharishi anointed me "the first Psychopath of new age."

Sudhir: The most worshipped teacher, what came next?

Swami: With Maharishi's blessings, I cured suffering individuals of all ages and from all walks of life. Many of them had tried all types of costly modern medicines but to no avail. As the news of my successes spread, sick men, women and children travelled from far and wide to receive treatment and returned home healthy. I thus earned the gratitude of a large proportion of country's population which had been suffering from a variety of ailments caused by extensive pollution of air and water due to rampant industrialisation. My popularity attracted the notice of bigwigs in country's main opposition party and they invited me to replace their error prone leader. However, being a humble servant of God, Maharishi and humanity at large, I resisted all pressures including my own temptation. Instead, following the wish of Maharishi, I am setting out to treat the ills of the western world with Psychopathy and free its people from the clutches of modern medicine.

Sudhir: The most worthy disciple, what is your goal?

Swami: My goal is to have native psychopaths available wherever human beings are suffering from ailments of body or spirit. Therefore, I now accept patients only if they are potential psychopaths and they are willing to undergo arduous training in my ashram.

Sudhir: The most sought-after Sanyasi, tell us about ashram and the life of disciples.

Swami: I am justly proud of the ashram which disciples built and furnished in the style prevalent in the heyday of psychopathy. The ashram is located near the confluence of three holy rivers where Buddha attained enlightenment. The spirit of sadhus (monks) of the past millenniums pervades the atmosphere. A large meditation room is the focal point of the ashram. This is surrounded by randomly placed and adequately furnished mud huts. Each hut has a straw mat to sleep on, an ankle-high stool for chair and a clay pot and a clay cup for water which disciples draw from the ashram well. The toilet facilities are open fields just as in good old days. The floor and walls of the meditation room are painted with fresh cow-dung every morning. Disciples sit on bare floor in sadhu-asana for meditation. The spray of cold water on straw roof scents the air in the room to counter the odour from bodies perspiring profusely in the heat of the tropical day. Both genders are welcome in the ashram. As befits a holy ashram, disciples live humbly and dress modestly in saffron clothes. Males have unkempt long hair and beards. Females follow the ancient devdasi (priestess) tradition and have cropped heads. Make-up is out of the question. Vegetarian meals consist of simple unspiced curries served with boiled rice or flat wheat bread sometimes supplemented by yoghurt or skimmed milk. Males and females, even the married couples, live in separate huts and maintain a respectful distance between themselves. Except for Kama Yoga practised in public by yogis (saints) and devdasis who have attained ultimate detatchment of body and spirit, sex is an offence that leads to immediate expulsion with no refund. Children have no place in this abode of peace and meditation and are not allowed even to visit.

Sudhir: The most admired master, how does psychopathy work?

Swami: The psychic powers developed after many years of meditation allow psychopaths to diagnose the sickness as soon as a patient comes into their presence. The instantaneous diagnosis instils confidence in the patient. The psychopaths build on this foundation by recommending a drastically simple lifestyle. The final elements in the cure are the medicines obtained from minerals and roots, bark and leaves of plants which are powdered in a holy bowl while chanting appropriate mantras. The basic materials are available everywhere if one knows what to look for. However, it takes years of hard work and meditation to develop psychic intuition and to learn of appropriate herbs and minerals and matching mantras to cure all that ails the humankind.

Sudhir: The most learned gurudeva, how does one train to become a psychopath?

Swami: It is a tough course and I have to pick disciples very carefully. They rise with the sun, practise yoga for an hour before breakfast and then meditate with me for rest of the morning. Afternoons are for self-meditation and repose. After a light evening meal, disciples gather for more yoga and meditation. Then they retire for much needed and well-deserved sleep. This regimen is followed strictly seven days a week for six weeks. Though many chose not to, disciples may visit the family for following two weeks but they must refrain from alcohol, tobacco, drugs and sex. I encourage them to spend most of this time in looking after their business affairs. After the disciples are cured of worldly ills, those devoted enough to have developed requisite psychic insight get thorough training in naturopathy. Finally, some qualify as psychopaths, receive a diploma in Psychopathy and become swamis themselves.

Sudhir: The most holy psychopath, what are your plans for new psychopaths?

Swami: After earning the diploma, a new psychopath signs a franchise agreement with my not-for-excessive-profit company and sets up a new ashram which must follow the original model as closely as local circumstances permit. The operating expenses and franchise fees are recovered from Psychopaths-in-training via dues which are set as a percentage of their present and future financial assets. This is why disciples are encouraged to manage their assets carefully for the good of all stakeholders.

Sudhir: The most insightful mahayogi, what are your travel plans?

Swami: If all stars are in harmony, I hope to visit North America later this year to select prospective disciples for treatment and training in my ashram. The successful trainees will provide Psychopathic healing as well as train more psychopaths.

Sudhir: (Touching Swami's feet with due humility) Thank you for your blessed words to our reader.

*****

Swami wishes me to inform the readers that meetings are being organised all across the continent to provide the opportunity of communing with His Holiness to as many devotees as possible. Please call 779 246 7284 (psy cho path) or visit the website: world.is my.oyster.forever for information.

# Friends, Really!

## 1

Ravi has an opinion on every subject under the sun. If you are talking about some obscure subatomic particle with a nuclear physicist he interrupts just as he would if you were talking about some strange illness in a remote tropical island. He is even more annoying because he is always right and experts are usually surprised by his knowledge. He is impressive at parties where he can deliver sermons on the glory of music by unheard of composers like Hummel as well as on the greatness of Beethoven's quartets. If literature is being discussed, he can deliver a lecture on the beauty of *Paradise Lost* and the depth of the novels of Margaret Atwood. He knows all about Field Hockey and Canadian Hockey, baseball and cricket, soccer and football. What amazes everybody is that his knowledge does not come from watching television. He hates the boob tube and leaves the room if it is turned on. He even watches the election results on radio.

The secret of the vast expanse of Ravi's knowledge is the newspaper. He devours the newspaper every morning at the age of seventy with the same ferocity as he did at the age of six. All political, sports and business news, all editorial comments and all published letters to the editors for the last sixty four years in every newspaper within his reach are stored in his brain cells in the language in which he read them. He can tell you why Anthony

Eden invaded Suez Canal and why Mao withdrew from Indian territory that his army had occupied. He can comment on every book, play, movie, even television program ever reviewed in the paper without having felt the urge to see or read any of them. If someone knowledgeable examines his loudly pronounced opinions, it becomes quite clear that they are being transmitted from a long forgotten source without any filtering by a moment's thought.

It is perhaps true that Ravi is like a lake with infinite parameter but very shallow depth. He "knows" about every thing but perhaps does not understand anything. That is why he is very popular among people with shallow interests but never got much respect in any of the numerous professions he pursued; he is admired by relative strangers but avoided by "friends". Not that it bothers him any. Being left alone undisturbed permits him to absorb thoroughly the contents of daily newspapers and his favourite magazines in print and now also on the web. Till recently, there was no sign of him running out of storage space in his head. Perhaps the thinking cells died of neglect and were replaced by storage cells. However, a while ago he lost interest in reading and could not understand why. Then it struck him, after seeing a cartoon on a greeting card, that his brain may be full. The stuff in his brain had to be reorganized to create new storage space. The only logical way to do it is by writing stories and essays. The sole purpose of writing by brainy people is to organize the information in the head, get rid of the duplicate or unnecessary stuff cluttering the brain and arrange what is important in an orderly fashion tightly packed in smaller space. This may not be true for many authors but there can be no other purpose in Ravi's writing if only because his subject matter is so dense, arguments so circuitous and style so boring that no one else can be expected to want to plough through it. Every editor he has sent his stories and essays to, and there have been many, has turned them down perhaps after reading the first two lines. Since the purpose of writing is not to be published or read, the insensitivity of editors does not bother him. It makes more cells available for newly read material. What else does he wish for?

Ravi was a quick reader in his younger days. For most of his life he read the newspaper before the rest of the family had opened their eyes. But as he got past his middle age, his eyes got weaker and his reading became slower. Although it never occurred to him, it may also have been due to the clogged brain with so many years of information thrown in randomly. In any event, now it takes him all morning and young ones have to wait for comics and sports till they finish school. As a result, they don't get new jokes for their friends and can't discuss games from the previous night intelligently without having read the views of sportswriters. The resentment is building up and the resolution of the problem is not in sight, not in Ravi's sight anyway.

It has been suggested that Ravi should take a page out of Somerset Maugham's book, not literally of course. He could do his writing in the morning, leaving the newspaper with others. This will create the extra space in his brain for new information to be absorbed from the paper in the afternoon. However, Ravi can't understand such complexities because he is short on thinking cells. His family is sponsoring research at the local medical school on just how to convert some spare storage cells into thinking cells. In the last meeting to discuss the renewal of the grant, researchers were cautiously optimistic, as behooves their profession. Till the research bears fruit, the family is taking delivery of two copies of the papers every morning.

2

Roberto was a well-known scientist, recognized all over the world for his work on alternative sources of energy. He had honorary doctorates conferred on him by five universities on three continents and is considered a likely Nobel winner every year. He realizes the importance of keeping his neurons active and his Naturopath wife has convinced him that a proper diet is essential to keep these cells orbiting in his brain without colliding with each other. Therefore, shopping every Saturday for groceries has become his passion, second only to writing letters to the media about dangers of using coal and hydrocarbons as energy sources. Of course, the passion does not stop him from using his car for pleasure and business and gas for keeping his home and office temperatures high enough to save wearing out his jackets.

This was a fine morning for shopping even though the super-store was crowded. Roberto was in great spirits, whistling his favourite Mahler melody while loading the cart with organic cucumbers, broccoli and tomatoes. Whole wheat bread, chunky granola, skimmed cottage cheese, plain yogurt and skimmed milk filled his cart to the brim. He was still whistling gaily the melancholy tune when he charged the groceries and accepted help to push the cart to his car. The store hired slightly challenged young men to help customers load their purchases in the car. They were not bright, but always cheerful and unfailingly polite and helpful; more than can be said of some store employees who laid claims to full use of their faculties. The badge told Roberto that his man was called Midge.

Roberto pressed the right buttons on his electronic key to open the trunk and the door of the car. He decided not to start the engine till Midge had finished loading to save him from the exhaust fumes. When Midge had finished and closed the trunk, Roberto put his hand in the right pocket of his top coat for the car keys, no luck. No luck with left pocket either. He got out of the car, looked into the pockets of pants and jackets, even the shirt; still no luck. He called out to Midge, "Midge, Midge, come back, help me unload the groceries, my keys must be in the trunk."

Midge walked back slowly, maneuvering the empty cart

carefully between throngs of stressed out shoppers. When he got close to Roberto he asked, "Sir, how can I help you?"

"Oh, my keys, they must be under the groceries. Will you help me find them?"

"Yes sir. They are in the ignition."

As Midge shuffled back, Roberto sheepishly pushed himself behind the wheel, wondering.

3

Early November is a quiet time for the bed and breakfast business in Banff, a mountain resort in the Canadian Rockies. The summer rush is over and the ski season has not yet begun. Alana doesn't mind this because her birthday falls at this time and she and her husband have a custom of a quiet candle light dinner to celebrate the occasion. Therefore, she was not at all happy when a travel agent called to book a room for the romantic evening. He spun out a long story of how both sets of parents had decided to descend on a young couple at the same time but they could accommodate only one of them in their home. The room was needed for the husband's parents who were very musical and loved to sing duets while playing the piano. Alana, the agent said, was referred to him by a mutual friend who knew of the concert grand in her living room. The visitors lived in the Black Forest area of Germany and would stay for two days before leaving for the mountains. Alana let herself be persuaded, particularly when the agent promised her that the couple would be going out for a family dinner. She did not ask any questions. What question could she ask when the agent was mailing the check in advance?

The check arrived the day before the German couple were due. The accompanying letter informed Alana that the guests were called Siegmund and Sieglinde Volsung. All her friends even with a drop of German blood, Aryan or Semitic, have one thing

117

in common – they are fanatics for order and cleanliness. "I will show them" Alana thought and got going with her vacuum cleaner, dusting brush, cleansing chemicals and polishing creams. She inspected their sheets and towels with and without her glasses under the strongest lights and ironed them till her arms ached. It was close to midnight before every nook and cranny was probably up to the exacting standards of a German hausfrau. When she finished after working nonstop for ten hours, Alana was tired but full of inner joy that comes with the feeling of contentment from a tough job well done. She dropped in bed and was sound asleep as soon as her head hit the pillow, totally oblivious of her husband's out of pitch snoring.

Alana cancelled her bridge meeting out of fear that the players would bring specks of dust into the living room. To keep the kitchen clean, she postponed the candle light dinner to the following week. She made sure the husband and the kids stayed a respectable distance away from the piano lest its shiny ebony surface was accidentally touched. The time went very slowly, as it does when you want it to pass quickly. Alana must have read the newspaper six times. She knew what was on sale and where, even though taking advantage of any of the sales would ruin her careful Feng Shui arrangement.

At last it was six, the time the guests were due to arrive. Alana was glad they were not staying for dinner. The young man had called to tell her that the guests would come in for a quick freshening before an elegant dinner of barbecued pheasant he was preparing. Alana had arranged for the kids to play with friends and the husband went out to shop for shirts. All by herself, she was a bundle of nerves not knowing whether to sit down and watch the news of yet another terrorist attack on TV or rearrange the flowers in the guest room one more time. Just when she was about to break into sweat, she heard the strains of familiar music, something from a film she had seen recently. Then the bell rang and she almost jumped out of her skin. She rushed to the front, stopped momentarily to force a smile on her face and opened the door to welcome her Germans.

Horror of horrors! What did she see? Two buffoons, animal skins draped over them, each carrying a cardboard sword, Viking helmets with long curved horns covering their long blonde hair which didn't look natural, the woman carrying a tape recorder playing *Ride of Valkyries*. Who are these idiots dressed for Halloween a week late? Why were they at her door when the guests were due any minute? Then the penny dropped. *Ride of Valkyries* – Wagner – *The Ring* – *Die Walkure* – Volsungs – Siegmund and Sieglinde. She had been had. She looked closely at the two heavily painted faces of the revelers. They were Laughingstocks, her dear friends who were known as practical jokers *par excellence*.

The dam burst and they all started laughing and hugging each other. They were still giggling like preteen girls half an hour later when Alana's husband returned. Pretend Vikings insisted they all go for the elegant dinner they had booked. There never was a dinner with as much laughter as that one. Laughter is contagious. Before long, every one in the dining room was laughing their heads off without knowing why.

In spite of all the hard work that went in preparation, Alana tells every one who would listen that there will never be another birthday like her twenty-ninth.

4

Waiparous is a small community of a few dozen homes located in a forestry reserve one hour of a picturesque drive away from Calgary. A gurgling mountain stream flows through the community. The water in the stream is not much warmer than ice; after all, that is what it was a few minutes earlier. A few of the homes are occupied all year round but most are summer cottages.

These are cottages in name only. They are large homes with three or more bedrooms and spacious living areas equipped with central heating, mega TVs and fireplaces. The owners and their families use them to show off their stature to business associates and make them available to clients in return for juicy contracts from their companies. However, there is one cottage in the heart of the community that cannot be glorified by such an elevated title. This is a cabin built sixty years ago by two tiny but determined and hardy ladies, modeled after the settler homes they were brought up in on far away Saskatchewan farms.

The cabin is still exactly as it was built; low beams ready to bounce off the head of any one taller than five feet, small windows on three sides and a door which even the builders must have stooped low to get through. Of course there is no electricity, water or telephone. Heating is by a wood stove. The current owners, a middle-aged couple we will call Eva and Dan, spend occasional weekends there in the summer when they use a camp stove to cook simple meals. As for winter, they slept there one November night. It took them three days to defrost after they somehow managed to get their frozen bodies home. Never again did they dare to go back to their cabin after the grass stopped growing on the lawn.

I am sorry if I have given a wrong impression. Eva and Dan were really fond of their cabin. They constantly thought of ways to make it comfortable while preserving its rusticity and historic authenticity. With these noble ends in mind, they often visited a store that catered to campers. It was on one such visit that they spotted what seemed like a panacea for somewhat boring summer afternoons in their cabin when the water in the stream was too cold for a swim and the outdoors is too cloudy to sunbathe. What they were looking at with their mouths wide open, believe it or not, was a box with the picture of a raft. The box said the inflatable raft it contained was big enough for two, was easily navigable, could handle shallow waters and was made of tough plastic.

Manufactures had thought of everything. Even a pedal pump was included. As if all that was not temptation enough, it was on sale, reduced to $99.99 from $109.99, plus tax of course. Such deals don't come by too often, not unless you search the papers for them all week, and Dan and Eva had no time for such frivolities. Before one could say "Done deal," the box was on the roof of the car, securely tied with ropes they carried in the car for such fortunate occasions.

To save the trouble of reloading, Dan left the box tied to the car roof till the weekend. It was a fine Saturday morning when Eva packed the picnic of their favourite egg salad sandwiches, cups of fruit yogurt, flasks of Earl Grey tea, juicy red apples and a bottle of cheap champagne to inaugurate the raft. With Mahler's *Song of the Earth* playing on CBC, they drove to their cabin anticipating the joyful ride from Waiparous to Ghost Lake and back. They expected it would take an hour downstream and a couple of hours back, just enough time for them to drive back home to watch the Stanley Cup playoff game on TV.

They unloaded the box, carefully opened it and removed the contents. The sun was warm, not a cloud in the bright blue sky and not even a whiff of breeze, ideal weather for their exciting venture. They spread out the circular plastic raft, making sure there were no thorns or sharp sticks on the ground to puncture it. It looked small for two, but they were small too. It may be just enough to squeeze in when inflated. After carefully reading all instructions in one language he understood of the nineteen they were printed in, Dan connected the pump to one of the six air intake points and started pumping. Soon he was sweating. Eva took over. She was wiping sweat off her brows when the first section was done. It took a few rest stops and longer time than they had anticipated but at last the boat was inflated. They let out a whoopee, changed into swim suits, put rubber sandals on, secured paddles in the boat, heaved it on to their shoulders and marched to the "beach" singing "*Saints go marching in*".

Several of the neighbours were enjoying the afternoon on their patios. Every one complimented them on the raft and wished them a good time. Dan and Eva carefully placed the raft next to the water. It took a while to find a spot where the rocks were not too sharp for the plastic and which was deep enough to launch their craft. Somehow they managed to find room for their legs as they sat on the blown up rim. The raft moved shakily forward, hit a shallow patch and stopped with a jolt. Dan lurched back, lost his balance and was soon lying in water. He scrambled up, pulled the boat in the deeper water and got in.

The boat hadn't gone ten feet when it hit another bump. It was Eva's turn to tumble over. The water was deeper now and Dan jumped out to help her. They were shivering in waist deep water when they noticed that the boat had drifted away. Eva swam to it and pulled it back.

I am not one of those who bask in *schadenfreude* and I don't believe my readers do. Therefore, I will skip their other attempts to get the boat into deeper waters. Enough to say that even souls as determined as our heroes give up once in a while. For them the last straw was when one of the paddles disappeared in a current. Shivering with cold and heads bowed in disappointment, they dragged themselves with the wretched boat on their shoulders to the cabin. Sunbathers saw them trudging up the street and mercifully kept their comments to a minimum.

Deflating the raft did nothing for the egos of Dan and Eva. It went back in the box, never to be seen again.


5


*A friend whose wife is an avid hiker kept a detailed diary of their hiking holiday in the Rockies. I present some of his notes to encourage you to join him next summer.*

҂

Day minus 170
Send the registration form and postdated cheque for first Skyline club hike. Make an elaborate plan to get fit.

Day minus 169
Shelve the plan.

Day minus 7
Wife reminds of the hike. Plan to get fit - walk up four floors to office twice a day. Stop on second floor to rest. Door to the elevator locked. Walk up stopping at each floor to recover breath. Collapse in the chair on reaching office.

Day minus 3
Walk up to third floor before resting. Get coffee before collapsing into chair.

Day minus 1
Pack folding bed and chair, sleeping bag and one spare pair each of underwear and socks. Still a little under specified weight. Pick a book for inevitable rainy day. Daughter sees it and screams, "Mom, Dad is reading his biography." The book is the Russian classic, *The Idiot*. Drove to a Canmore hotel in a very foul mood.

Day - 0
Bag overweight by one ounce. Take out extra pair of underwear, will turn inside out what I have on after three days. Partake dinner of steak fit to make hiking boots. Meet a renowned psychiatrist in the hot tub who declares that masochism and sadism are two sides of the same personality.

Day - 1
On the grueling 20 km long hike on a muddy trail, grade masochists and sadists. At the low end are masochists who hike flat dry trails for a few kilometers. Corresponding sadists are the leaders* who stop every few yards to explain the beauties of Rocky Mountain dandelions when mosquitoes are sucking out hikers' blood. The other end of spectrum are the masochists who start on

a 20 km long tough hike without any physical training and sadists who are determined to lead these poor hikers to camp in time for dinner. Last hiker to enter the camp, just ahead of tailender's* boot. Not late for dinner - dinner delayed for the slow pokes. Campsite located on the bank of a gurgling stream in a beautiful meadow surrounded by beautiful mountains. Ecstasy overtakes weariness.

Day - 2

Easy hike to a glorious lake. The leader scares a grizzly and spoils a photo op for our southern visitors. Wife and I rest on the beach for two hours watching loons and a pair of bald eagles in between some crafty moves in a game of Scrabble when rest of the group visits a waterfall. Lose, in spite of a hefty bonus for English being second language. Uneventful evening. Once in sleeping bag, share some stale jokes with tent mates, a young couple from Ontario. Jokes send them snoring in a hurry.

Day - 3

Awake at 4 AM, thanks to a rather loud growl. Alarmed but decide to investigate before disturbing others in the tent. Growl turns out to be rather sonorous snoring from the tent behind. Go back to snoring myself – totally relaxed. Miss the wake-up bell and breakfast. On the return trip from aptly named Zorro falls, try to improve the recluse image. A most interesting conversation with the couple from Deep South – in sign language. Group rushes back to camp to avoid hungry mosquitoes to welcome cups of tea in the dining tent. Proceed to my tent to be greeted by the biggest swarm of starving mosquitoes ever assembled. Bites offset by the standard aromatherapy treatment for tired bodies and aching limbs – the glorious scents wafting in the gentle breeze from five outhouses strategically located to take full advantage of prevailing winds in the valley.

---

*The leader leads the way and sets the speed from the front and the tail-ender stays at the back to make sure no one is left behind.*

Day - 4

Decide to wrest control of my body from aches and pains by resting for the day in the camp. Rest and aromatherapy rejuvenate the spirits and can face the thought of 20 km return trip day after next. Will go on a gentle hike of 12km the next day to get back in shape. Read enough of *The Idiot* to find that the idiot was the model of future Russian heroes. This explains the misery in Russia since the book was published in 1870.

Day - 5

Start the day on the wrong foot – again. Hear the rumour at breakfast that I am to be with a faster group on the return trip tomorrow. Not because I have improved, but because the leader of the slowest group would not accept this East Indian who does not take orders from his Chief and who can't talk and walk uphill at the same time - whether chewing gum or not. All's well that ends well. Humble apologies on bended knees restore my coveted status as the slowest hiker in the camp. It is not the end of my woes though. The leader for today's "easy" hike appoints me the tail-ender of the small group, apparently because I will be lagging behind anyway. When I extend my hand for the tail-ender's whip, the leader refuses because I will be too far behind others for it to be of any use.

Day - 6

The ten hour return trip to trailhead uneventful except for scorching sun and trauma due to leader's rush to get there before the fastest group who left camp two hours later. Avoided tail-ender's whip because another member of the group twists his ankle and has to be physically supported. Frequent stops to prevent dehydration and sunstroke only partially successful. Lie low with mild headache on the drive home.

Day - 7

Back home, spend the day cleaning up self and airing the camping gear. Things put away out of sight and out of mind till masochistic fervour takes hold again. For now, ecstasy of a week in natural surroundings offset by the agony of aching muscles and itching mosquito bites. Hopefully, agony will soon pass but ecstasy will remain. Fitter or worse, I shall return.

∞

6

"We can still be friends," Sam's brand new ex-wife said. He was dumbstruck. He could not respond because he did not know how. Diane's dramatic flair had won Sam's heart for ever. At least he thought so when he was young and foolish and they were in Senior High. She used this talent with great effect to stump Sam's lawyer and melt the heart of the judge. His Honour was like putty in her deft hands. She convinced him that Sam had been a lousy husband and father. He rejected, after careful deliberation, he said, Sam's version of the events that he had left a good job to look after their two children when Diane decided to go to the medical school, and that they had used his inheritance and savings to survive eight lean years of her training. The judge was taken in by her tearful testimony that Sam was a lazy bum who constantly complained about his desk job with a major oil company and was glad to have an excuse to stay at home and watch soap, that he never cooked a meal or vacuumed the floor, never took the kids to soccer or even cut the grass, leave alone mend the roof and that poor Diane had to cope with all the chores of a busy household along with the heavy load that a medical student carries. Soon to be his ex added insult to injury by implying, without being direct, on her crafty lawyer's advice, that the only reason Sam got the job as a medical orderly in the local hospital where she delivered babies was to make her feel bad, not because she refused to make him an allowance for a smoke and an occasional visit to the bar after his savings had run out. She even said under oath that Sam had threatened to hit her when all he had said was that he is having difficulty controlling himself while raising his hand.

Sam did not mind her being granted the divorce; good riddance some would say, though he would never be that crude. He did mind the judge siding with her to the extent that he was deprived of his half of the marital property on the grounds that her earnings had paid for it. He lost his home in the swanky suburb, the La-Z-Boy that his back had grown accustomed to, Rod Stewart albums that he loved to play at full volume, and a collection of rare eighteenth century erotica which he loved to hear Diane read aloud. To rub salt in the wounds, Sam will have to pay most of his meager earnings in child support. He must find shelter, buy necessities of life and entertain the children for three hours a week the generous judge has allowed him, all on less than a tenth of what he became used to as a doctor's spouse.

Sam told me this story with tears in his eyes. Then his face became red and his voice became shrill. "She says we can be friends! Ha! Maybe one day when I have won the super lotto, better still, won my appeal to the higher court."

7

I am Asha. I am a fifteen months old baby girl. As long as I can remember, I have lived in this home with my Momma, her partner Roshan, my four year old sister Kahlo, Grammy and Grumpy. Jessica looks after me for four days every two weeks when my Momma is away. I know they all love me in their own ways. I love them too. But being so much in demand, I have established an order of preference among them, a pecking order if you like. I insist that they know their place and keep to it if only because I cannot be fed, changed, cuddled or put to bed by all of them simultaneously.

Jessica is kind and loving, but she is on the bottom rung of the ladder. The reason should be obvious even to a grown up. She is only with me for four days, and only during the day time, and then away for ten days. I am only a baby with a short memory. All her love and kindness slip away from my mind during her absence. It is like meeting someone new every other Monday. Even if I could remember, I have to be practical. If I loved her more, I would miss her terribly during her absence and this would be hard on my preemie baby heart. I readily grant you that she couldn't look after me better when she is here. But she will have to be with me more often to climb higher on the fan ladder.

Sister Kahlo is next. I can see that she loves me most of the time. However, her inconsistency is perplexing. She complains when I am receiving Momma's attention even though I need it more than her. I would never do that when I have a baby sister, neither should she. I could understand her selfishness, after all she is only four and humans are born to be selfish. That is why Grumpy rails against selfishness but to no avail. But I can't understand why she pushes me against the hard marble floor when nobody is looking. When I cry and adults tell her off, rightly if you ask me, her screams shake the house to the rafters. After a lot of cajoling she sheds crocodile tears and says sorry and, no doubt, starts planning her next scheme to punish me for the crime, in her eyes, of being here. I observe all this and store it in my baby mind. There is a lot of time for revenge, a whole childhood lies in front of us. I am afraid, there is no chance dear sister can climb the ladder. I have a suspicion she doesn't want to either.

Roshan comes next. From what I gather from their whispers when they think I am asleep, Roshan is not well and needs a lot of looking after. She is in direct competition with me and sister Kahlo for Momma's attention. I can stand this for a while because she is not well. But she will slip down the ladder if she doesn't get well before long. In my baby heart I feel sure that she will soon be better and the day is not far when she is sharing the top rung.

Grammy is next. Grammy works hard to look after everybody. She prepares lovely meals and everybody goes ooh and aah when they are enjoying them. I enjoy them too, much more than the bottle I am fed all the time. Grammy also looks after the sick. She examines me by putting a warm metal disc on my body, nods wisely and prescribes what she calls auntie Biotics although the only real aunties I have are auntie Boofie and auntie Kamini. Grammy is my favourite also because she really genuinely cares for me and my well-being. If she were not so busy with all the things she has to do, she will have more time to cuddle me and then she will climb right to the top rung.

Grumpy is next to the top because he has all the time in the world to pick me up, cuddle me, talk to me, tell me stories when he gives me the bottle, and most important, pat me on the back and tummy when he is putting me to bed. If he slinks out when I am not quite into the dream world, my slightest whimper pulls him again to my cot and he pats my back, rubs my tummy and talks to me till I finally fall asleep. His talk is very soothing but honestly I don't know what it all means. It does show that he cares for me in his own dumb way. I really like him and he will stay near the top as long as he doesn't get over-confident and starts treating me with less attention. If he does that, he has a long way to fall. He should beware if he doesn't want to get hurt.

Top rung is Momma, of course. I know that without her I would still be a soul circling the Earth looking for a body to move into. She went to endless trouble to secure my soul, then nurture it in her tummy, bring it into the world and then nourish it into a healthy baby body. I miss her terribly when she is away although family down the ladder work hard to make up and they do to some extent. But darling Momma is irreplaceable, her cooing and cuddling is special. Her love is transparent even when she is annoyed. I would rather snuggle closer to her when she is upset with me then slink away quietly like adults do.

This is my list. There is always room on the ladder for newcomers. Application forms are on Baby Union's website. Accepted applicants will start at the bottom. I will evaluate their effort at regular intervals and assign them the proper place. A note of warning: Competition is stiff and faint of hearts need not apply.

8

Our daddy had a wonderful life. He had a devoted wife, three loving daughters and four cute granddaughters. He was a successful consultant till he had enough of chasing business. Then he became an investor and helped in growing the savings of the family members and friends. And in between throwing darts at investment boards he wrote letters. Not to us, we only got one line e-mail messages once in a blue moon. He wrote letters to the editors of newspapers and magazines. He wrote about business, politics, social affairs and even medicine. But Mom put a stop to medical pronouncements by insisting that she approve them first. We could never understand why, but editors seemed to like his letters. National and local newspapers published them once a week till other letter writers complained. Then he was restricted to one letter a month and editors installed filters to block his letters for 30 days after accepting a letter. Just as well they did.

Daddy was very proud of his published letters. He emailed them to every body he knew and they promptly deleted them, often without reading. Not only that, he saved in a box the whole page of the newspaper with the letter and, if it was a magazine, the whole magazine. Not only did he keep letters, he kept anything else that was published with his name. Response to letters which, thankfully, were rare, published puns howsoever bad, accepted entries in *Globe Challenge* and other columns were all stored. He also photocopied his successes and filed them in binders. For a while he toyed with the idea of publishing them in a book but the response, rather the lack thereof, from prospective publishers soon put paid to that idea.

It took a couple of years to fill the first box; only a year to fill the next one. He had found a way to break the once-a-month restriction. No, not pseudonyms. He did try them but was caught and had to stop for fear of being blacklisted. He made a list of all Canadian newspapers available on the Internet. He wrote to them in turn and got published a couple of times a week in papers he would never see. He printed the published version from the internet and stored a copy in the box and filed another in a folder. After a few years there was no room for the boxes and folders at home. He found a self-storage company and persuaded them to offer him discounted terms for the depositary of historical interest. Mom did not like parting with the money that could be useful in so many ways but did not want to upset a husband who was showing signs of dotage.

Daddy passed away of a stroke when he was writing a letter, yes, a letter to the editor. I am certain that this is the end he would have wished. Only he would have wished to pass away after submitting the letter. But poor Marlene got so upset when she saw him slumped on the keyboard in his office that she accidentally deleted the file and the world will never know what his last words were. However, the world does know his second last words; they were published in Nunavut Express on page A21 in the bottom right hand corner; twenty one words, not counting his name, about a polar bear being shot.

Mom says she is getting too old to look after family memorabilia and it is time for us sisters to divide them between us. There is no problem dividing jade statues, brass elephants or antique Buddha and the fire screen. However, who wants those boxes of old papers smelling of age? If they contained works of art, some memorable writing, wisdom of ages, we would be fighting for them. But letters! Particularly letters written to be published – not even expressing his views, without any developed logical arguments, on issues of the day with no lasting interest. Who would want them? Even if one of us got sentimental and wanted them for memory's sake, would she dare to open the boxes and inhale the stale air of the twentieth century? Yet, if we all refused to take them Mom will feel hurt thinking that we are desecrating the memory of a good husband and a good father, at least till he got bitten by the letter bug.

A possible solution to the problem might be to donate them. Some library somewhere may value the collection of letters published over thirty years on hot topics of the day so long as we don't give the impression that the letters did not always express his true opinion. It may even be a good topic for research by a graduate student. We may have to offer a fellowship for the student and some travel grant for the professor to tempt them to team up. It is worth checking into. There were a few dollars left in his retirement fund last we looked into it.


9


Salim's work as a cab driver is hard but not without compensation. The hours are long but not necessarily boring. In between passengers he has time to work out in his mind the outlines of amusing stories he likes to write for the enjoyment of his family and friends. Purely by accident, he left one of these on the back seat a few weeks ago. A bookish type passenger read it and suggested he submit it for publication. Thus encouraged, he sent it to the editor of his community magazine. He felt that it was good to start at the bottom and establish a publishing record before attacking the appropriate venues for his literary work. Another positive in his job is that the passengers are often interesting. He serves people in all walks of life from all corners of the world. Businessmen traveling alone can be a drag because as soon as the seatbelt is fastened, blackberry comes out and they are connecting to the bosses or the bossed with the results of the latest meeting. It is funny how they feel free to discuss the most confidential matters completely oblivious of two ears in the front taking in everything. If they think that the cabbies are bound by some code of ethics, no one told Salim about it. But he does feel honour bound not to broadcast the latest twists in the hot takeover battles although he is not beyond whispering the critical details in well heeled ears, for appropriate tip of course. As for benefiting from such information by indulging in stock market activity, he keeps away from it. Firstly it is illegal to trade on confidential information; secondly he doesn't have any money left after paying for the gas.

A few weeks ago, all these considerations were thrown out of the passenger side window. Two fellows with loaded not-so-brief cases hailed Salim and jumped in giggling to themselves. The cell phones came out and both started talking whether to their clients or bosses, Salim couldn't tell. With both talking at the same time it was hard to make out what they were saying. It seemed important and he strained his ears without appearing indiscreet. He did not understand the details but this much was clear: they had just negotiated a deal which would give the bondholders of a company in receivership full value for their money instead of twenty five cents in the dollar the bonds were trading at. The opportunity to quadruple the money in a few weeks looked too good to pass. Only problem was that old cliché: you need money to make money. After depositing the informants at the airport, Salim parked the car at a remote taxi stand where he could think with little chance of interruption. The owner of the taxi company was a gambler and spent all his time checking his portfolio. However, he was a skinflint. He would use the information, but he wouldn't even thank Salim let alone share the profits. Salim knew that Jamila, his wife, had been saving for a trip home. But she never told him where she secreted the money and there was no way he could find out without leaving telltale signs. The only possibility was Alibaba, the owner of the pawn shop in the community. According to rumours Alibaba lent you the money at hundred percent interest and ten percent fees to be paid in advance. He got his money with interest even from the hardest cases without ever going to court. The muscular collectors he hired were more efficient.

Even if he paid the standard interest and fees, Salim calculated that he would more than double the money. He drove straight to the pawn shop and asked Alibaba to lend him a couple of grand for something urgent. To his credit, Alibaba did not ask the reason. He took Salim to a dingy room in the back and told him the terms, "You are borrowing 2,500, including 500 in fees which are paid in advance and you have twelve months to pay me back 5,000. A year from today, Big Bull will call on you and if the money is not there, the consequences would not be pleasant for you or the family."

Salim did a quick calculation; 2,000 becomes 8,000, I give him 5000. That leaves 3,000, enough for a deposit on his own cab. "It is a deal," he said. They shook hands and he left the shop with twenty dirty hundred dollar bills. However, dirt didn't have time to stick to his fingers. Within a few minutes, bills had been converted into 8,000 dollar bonds.

The business news now became Salim's main interest. His car radio was turned on to the business channel. At home he disregarded Jamila's protests and turned the TV on to the Report on Business station. The company's restructuring was big news. A week later the deal on bonds was reported. The bonds shot up to 80 cents. He calculated that if he sold then he could walk away with 1,400. "Not enough for the deposit, a good investor must be patient," he remembered the advice of the Guru on the channel. A week later the bonds crashed to 20c. He was perplexed. There was no news but there must be some reason for such a fall. He called the company. After being kept waiting for a long time, enough to miss two fares, Salim was connected to an accountant type. He told Salim something about senior bonds claiming all the money and leaving little for Salim's junior bonds. Salim didn't follow the gobbledygook but his heart sank. Something was seriously wrong.

The due date came and went without any money showing up. Salim called the accountant directly. He said that the two types of bondholders are taking the matter to court. The case will be heard in two months and the judge will issue his verdict a month later. He said things didn't look good for "juniors," they may not get anything. Then he gave Salim the number of the lawyer representing juniors. The lawyer happened to be one his regulars and was very friendly. He was much more hopeful but he had another wrinkle, "The judgment will almost certainly be appealed by the losing side and it may not be settled for years." Just when Salim was going to collapse, he heard, "But it may be settled out of court too." Salim gave him his number and lay down on the backseat till the cop ordered him to move.

Salim received a call three months later, "I have just received the judgment. We have lost the case. I will call you again after I have studied the document." His world went dark. He owed Alibaba five grand and there was no way he could repay it. However, he still had eight months to plan his strategy. "Maybe my story will be published; some publisher will read it and offer me an advance for my book." Crazy thoughts, but these were his only hope. He spent the day in a daze, taking passengers to the wrong addresses and receiving deserved scolding from them. After work he walked up the stairs to his apartment pondering his next move. Fortunately, Jamila was wrapped in her own concerns, something about her kid sister in Lahore wanting to immigrate to Canada. Then his heart took a leap. There on the table was the letter from the Editor. He tore it open. Just one line, "Your story was not considered suitable for our journal." Salim felt his world was coming to an end for sure.

Salim is as resilient as the next man. Next morning he got up earlier than usual and drove to the taxi stand at the Grand Hotel. Who should come out of the hotel but the lawyer of the "juniors." He looked happy for someone who had lost a big case. He settled himself into the back seat without looking at Salim, took out his cell and dialed a number. Salim's cell rang and he heard in both his ears, "I was hasty calling you yesterday. We did lose the case but only partially. The judgment allows us fifty cents and will not be appealed. You should get your money in a few days." Salim thanked the caller and quickly worked out that he would be one grand short. Working two shifts over weekends for next eight months should make up this difference. "Allah is great, he teaches us lessons in the form we can learn," he thought. He said a silent prayer when the car was facing east. He now had another proof that Allah looks after the poor and the meek.

## 10

Vijay told me his story a long time ago and some of what I tell may not have actually happened. He had immigrated to Canada from India with a degree in Drama and Fine Arts. To get by, he drove a cab all day and looked for a job in his profession in the evenings. Gods must have been in a benevolent mood one snowy afternoon in November. He picked up a fare at the High Season hotel to take him to the Airport. When he opened the door for the tall well-groomed gentleman, he felt the power of a unique personality. It transpired that his guest was none other than Dr. Robertson, renowned for his work on the performance of medieval plays. He was familiar with the name as Dr. Robertson's fame had spread far and wide, even to his Backwater University back in India. The

Doctor was pleased when Vijay told him so. After checking him out with some searching questions, Dr. Robertson offered to interview Vijay for a research position in his department at Calgary School of Fine Arts. To make the long story short, Vijay joined his staff three months later. The job promised to be exciting: research in the staging of sixteenth century plays focusing on differences in modern presentation compared to what the playwright intended. It paid enough to live on and Vijay spent all his working time in the vaults of local libraries studying dramas written in the heyday of stage in England, sixteenth and seventeenth centuries. He absorbed the plays and read what the critics had to say about the performances and the performers. Life couldn't be better, not for a brownie cab driver from India anyway.

Well, it did become better. He won a bursary, thanks to the recommendation of Dean Robertson. The bursary was for him to spend six months to study original manuscripts of old plays preserved in British libraries. He was to travel to different libraries, find plays which were rarely performed, study them and make recommendations on any that should be revived. He walked on air for a few days. Then the enormity of the task hit home and he was rather nervous when the plane landed in Manchester. The hospitality of the local people and the warmth of greetings by the librarians soon set him at ease and he got down to work examining the pearls collecting dust in the archives.

On one such visit to a provincial university, Vijay found a well-preserved manuscript of a play in a musty cupboard. He had not seen this play mentioned before, not even heard the name of the author. The handwriting was poor and occasionally the ink had faded. But it was not difficult to guess the undecipherable words to suit the context. He spent a few weeks studying the text. The more he looked into it more he liked it. He decided that a simple staging, as would have been done by the playwright in his day, would be most effective. Therefore, it could be done at minimal cost. He surreptitiously copied the manuscript word by word and felt that the goal of his visit had been fully accomplished.

After returning to Calgary, he put together a group of enthusiastic students and gave them copies of the play to read. The prospect of performing a play they had never heard of but which made sense excited them. Due to various commitments of the group, the work was slow but steady. They experimented with the roles in workshops and finally settled on best actors for each part without acrimony. There were many qualified students ready to undertake the backstage work. Six months after the discovery of the play, the rehearsals began.

It took another six months of serious team work to have the play ready for performance. All Fine Arts public performances had to be approved by the Dean. When Vijay met with Dr. Robertson to discuss it, the Dean was more interested in how Vijay found the manuscript than in their work and was most upset that it had not been brought to his attention earlier. He demanded the manuscript so that he could study it himself before granting approval. Scared of losing his job, Vijay apologized profusely and handed him the original copy.

Vijay waited with bated breath for the call, fully expecting to return to his old job any day. Two weeks had gone by when Dr. Robertson's secretary called with the date and time of the meeting. All his fears were put to rest when the Dean greeted him warmly. He congratulated Vijay for discovering the lost manuscript of the work of Steadyapple, a seventeenth century playwright of some promise who died young. He emphasized that the performance of this work will attract wide attention among academic community and further enhance the already considerable reputation of the school. Therefore, they had to be careful about how it was presented. He asked Vijay to make sure he was present at the next rehearsal.

Vijay was relieved to note that the Dean was quite pleased with the performance. All participants were heartily complimented. The Dean did make a few suggestions on lighting and the diction of the main actors. He told Vijay to leave logistical arrangements with him. He was true to his word. The date was set, dignitaries were invited, posters were printed and an elaborate program was prepared. Vijay was spared the work in all these chores to focus on fine tuning the performance.

A week before the performance Vijay happened to see a poster in a shopping mall. It listed the main actors in bold letters and supporting cast in smaller type. The School of Fine Arts was highlighted as the producer. A large tobacco company was listed as the sponsor. To his consternation, the name of the director was left out. The reason became clear when he saw the program on the performance evening which listed the Dean as the director. It was too late for Vijay to complain without hurting the morale of the performers. He could do nothing but smile ruefully as the Dean received the compliments from the dignitaries. The critics praised the performance and complimented the Dean on his sensitive direction of a difficult work. Vijay was mentioned in passing as a young researcher who had accidentally come across the manuscript in a British library.

Vijay missed out on fame but did have the satisfaction of promoting young Steadyapple three hundred years after his death. The Dean had the satisfaction of promoting himself. What the Dean felt in his soul is something only he knew and lived with. Thanks to the critical acclaim the performance received, Steadyapple became quite fashionable with researchers, if not the public. However, like all academic fashions, this too ran out of steam after a few doctorates. Only mention of the playwright in recent years that Vijay noticed was in the obituary of Dr. Robertson proclaiming his discovery to be the late Dean's greatest achievement.

# Two sides of a coin

## 1

It was twenty years ago when I went looking for a new car. During the previous week, my ten year old jalopy had sputtered and died on my way to work. Not only was I acutely embarrassed trying to get help in the mad rush hour traffic, I was also a couple of hours late for work. An important client was in a foul mood because he had been waiting for quite a while. He told me in no uncertain terms that any excuse is good only once. In other words, get a reliable car, buster, or kiss my business goodbye.

My six year old daughter Alice insisted on accompanying me in search of an affordable new car. Flord had a good model but it appeared pricey, Crysome had an affordable car but it looked cheap, Colonel Motors had several affordable cars but the salesmen were too busy selling expensive models. Japanese cars were small but not affordable. Volkswakin and Wolso cars had to be ordered. I was frustrated and ready to give up when I came to a Merceles Band dealership. Maybe because I could not afford a luxury car, I always believed that a car was a car and shouldn't cost more than a house. However, Alice insisted on going in and I went along to humour her.

The first car we saw was a small two-seater priced to consume my earnings over a life-time. There was a shiny black limousine designed to be a house and priced like a mansion. In between, there was a blue sedan with beige leather seats sitting there with open doors. Like any normal six year old, Alice hopped in and started jumping on the seat. "Daddy, I like it, you must get it. Mom will be so happy to ride in it." I looked at the price sticker. "Priced to sell, 25% off, open to offers", it said. A soft cough broke my reverie. "You are welcome to take it for a drive sir, I will fetch the key." A couple of minutes later, I was in the car trying to maneuver it out of the show room and onto the road.

A few minutes on the road convinced me that someday I should own a car like this. Alice was even more impressed. She looked as if she had been transported to her wonderland. She was jumping up and down with joy, "our new car, our new car" as I drove the car back to the dealership. I asked Alice to come out but she refused. Tact, bribe, threats all failed. The salesman returned, "How was the drive, sir." "It is somewhat noisy, it vibrates a fair bit, probably won't start in cold weather," I said trying to wriggle out of the trap. "It is a diesel sir. It won't vibrate after the engine warms up. It is so well insulated that you don't hear any noise inside the car. It starts like a charm if you plug it in for a few minutes on cold mornings. Consider this: its running costs are less than half of even a small Japanese import." To enhance the impact of last line, he threw a well rehearsed clincher, "It is a million mile engine, sir. It lasts for ever. All taxies in Europe are this model."

I was defeated but not blind to my financial limitations. "OK, I will make you an offer. You make it 50% off, and I will discuss it with my wife." He disappeared for what felt like hours to discuss "the offer" with the manager. When he returned, he was beaming. "Manager is off his rocker today. He will accept your offer, so long as it is cash." I was flabbergasted. No way could I raise so much cash. And all this time Alice was in her wonderland jumping with joy, "Daddy's new car, Daddy's new car." I had to do something to get out of this jam. "No cash. You have signs all over saying zero percent financing over five years. This is a long life car. So I will take it at this price with your financing rate, but spread over ten years." The salesman looked at me as if I was from the moon, not a suburb west of Calgary. "The manager is not going to accept that. I will try though. I need a sale, if I am to keep this job." He disappeared again for so long that Alice came out of wonderland asking when we could have lunch. The salesman must have heard it. He rushed back, "Manager has to call the owner." If I could wait another few minutes, he would have the answer. I told him that I will be back after feeding my little girl.

The salesman and the manager were waiting for me next to the car. "Do you have a trade in?" the manager asked gruffly. "Yes, if you want it. You can pay for its funeral." The manager controlled his fury admirably, told the salesman to get the papers ready, get me to sign the pink slip of the old car, shook my hands and disappeared into his office to cry his heart out. An hour later, I drove into our driveway in a spanking new blue Merceles.

## 2

*I had just put the breakfast dishes away when the phone rang. Bob wanted to come and iron out some wrinkles in my appeal for admission to the University that day. My husband Kesh and our daughter Alice were out for a while, so I invited Bob and Laura to come over for tea in a couple of hours. My beloved family had not returned when the couple showed up. I was becoming a little anxious about their safety because Kesh's car had been giving trouble of late. But I put a brave face and resolved the issues with Bob over a few cups of strong Indian tea. They were putting on their coats when we heard a rumble in the driveway. Then Alice ran in screaming "Daddy's new car, Daddy's new car." Kesh followed in her footsteps and announced proudly, "I bought a Merceles."*

We went out and saw a beautiful blue car blinding onlookers with its shine. Bob and Laura paid the car due compliments. I felt a knife go through my heart. "How could this husband of mine spend a fortune on a luxury car for himself when we were barely scraping by?" I asked myself. Laura asked Kesh how much he had paid for it. The sum he mentioned twisted the knife full circle. My husband was prepared to throw away all our savings without discussing it with me. Was I just a chattel here to accept whatever was thrown at me, or a wife who had an equal say in decisions that affected the family? And he is showing me my place when I am in a fight for my career!

I won my appeal and in due course completed my degree. Kesh invited all of our friends for dinner at a local restaurant to celebrate the occasion. I got an inkling from Alice that he was planning to present me the key of his prized car on this occasion. I told him firmly that he was not to do anything of the sort. It would embarrass me to drive that showy car and might create an unfavourable impression among my colleagues. But the dear husband of mine has a habit of going deaf when it suits him. He did embarrass me by presenting the key. My best friend rubbed it in by saying that she thought it was a brand new model rather than an old one, no matter in perfect condition.

I drove the car for a while and then returned it on the pretext that I needed a station wagon. He got his pride back and bought a new suit to show off his expanded chest. The years rolled by and the car started showing its age like its owner. But Kesh was too proud to notice it. The reason was obvious to every one but him – his business was not doing well and he could not afford another luxury model. He could not, would not, drive an affordable car after owning Merceles for so long.

3

My new car sounded like a truck. Eva, my kind and considerate wife, said that it gave her enough notice of my arrival to hide any evidence of unsavoury activity. But it was luxuriously appointed and I felt like a company president when driving it. I actually was the president of a one person operation barely ekeing out a living. But the car presented an aura of success; rather, it announced success from a long way off.

But my fortunes turned. Business picked up. Soon I felt I deserved the car. But it didn't take long for success to go to my head. I spent the company's extra cash on a new office building. Then I hired employees to fill the building. At first, there was enough work to keep them busy. But all good things come to an end. One day almost all of my business contacts were shown the door, either with golden parachutes or forced into early retirement with hefty pensions. My revenue base collapsed. I had no alternative but to close shop, sell the building and live off my doctor wife's moral earnings.

In all this upheaval my Merceles Diesel stayed completely loyal. With minimum maintenance at a local gas station, it took me wherever I wanted to go, whether at the height of summer or in the depth of winter. Behind its wheel, I felt the pride of a man who had achieved professional success even when charging diesel to my wife's card. I also felt that no harm could reach me inside the car. The car was built of solid steel like a tank. Then, out of clear blue skies, the death knell thundered. One cold morning after a skiing weekend in the Rockies, the car refused to start even though it had been plugged in for the night. It took several hours to get it going. In the process, it let out a huge cloud of smoke with pungent fumes to darken the whole parking lot. The combination of delayed start and polluted mountain air was too much for Eva. She decreed that the car had to go. I pointed out that the trouble occurred only because the plug- in was not working and this problem will not arise again. She listened patiently and said nothing more. When we got home, she calmly pointed to the garage door behind my car which was charcoal grey while that behind her car was lily white.

The walls and ceiling of the garage on my side graded from grey to white from back to front. Her decision was final. The offending car had no place in our garage.

I was shattered. I would have to part with the only remaining sign of my past success. I had no money to replace it other than by cashing my retirement fund. This seemed a little short-sighted so I let matters slide. But matters did not slide for long.

A special birthday of my wife was approaching. Alice, now a grown up young lady of independent means, arranged a big birthday bash for her mother at a local restaurant and invited all her friends to shout surprise as she entered. Eva was greatly moved and gave me credit for this exceedingly pleasant party. I did not contest.

4

*On our way to a concert one evening, I noticed that the black leather of the dashboard was somewhat uneven and the glass next to the air vent was covered by a layer of soot. I drew my finger across the dashboard. The dashboard had a bright black line and my finger a thick encrustation of black powder some of which fell on my white dress. I showed Kesh my finger and asked where the stuff could have come from, how long had he been breathing the foul air, and what it had it to his lungs? He was dumbfounded. He said he would check with the mechanic the next time the car was being serviced. I suggested that the car be serviced before the week was over unless he wanted me to take the matter in my own hands.*

*The car was serviced. The mechanic gave it a clean bill of health and I thoroughly cleaned the interior of the car. The air through the vent was less polluted but not healthy by any means. As usual, Kesh continued to disregard my complaints. But my problems with the car had just begun. One morning I was woken up with a start. There were strange noises downstairs. I rushed down and opened the door from the family* room to the garage. The whole garage was full of black smoke which now poured into the house. It transpired that my darling husband had forgotten to plug in the car the night before and the process of starting the diesel engine in subzero temperature had woken me up and filled first the garage, and now the house with this poisonous air. Before I could express my frustration, the car left the garage and the door closed trapping the fumes in. I opened all the windows and doors in the house to let the freezing air replace warm carbon oxides and called the culprit on his cell. As gently as I could, I gave Kesh a piece of my mind. I relented and wished him a good day after he promised to get rid of the car as soon as possible.

When the smoke had cleared and I could breathe again, I peeped into the garage. I couldn't believe it. There was a film of black soot on every item in there – my car, bicycles, skis, freezer, tools, paint cans and garbage cans. The ceiling on his side was dark grey and light grey above my car. I had to leave early for work to get the car washed before the green car became permanently grey. I called Kesh from work and advised him that it will be good for family harmony for him to get home early and clean up the garage and to make sure that the car was parked on the other side of the street.

He took the car to his old faithful mechanic. The mechanic confirmed the problems with exhaust, ventilation system and starting solenoid. He estimated that the repairs will cost about the same as a new Rolls Royce. Kesh came home and sheepishly told me this tale of woe. After dinner, he made up For Sale signs and stuck them on all windows. I noticed with consternation that the signs were written with pale blue felt on light green paper. Only a mind reader could decipher the numbers. So I was not surprised that there was no response. A combination of black fumes, deafening engine noise and invisible signage was not very inviting. So, Kesh kept driving his pride and joy and I kept fuming in my heart as much as his car was fuming on the road.

My birthday was approaching and I felt a surprise party in the air. I decided to spring my own surprise. I offered to buy Kesh a brand new

*car of his choice if he would put his old clunker in deep freeze. His joy
at my offer overshadowed his pride and joy being called a clunker. He
spent a week on Internet search, then a week at various dealerships test
driving Flords, Crysomes, Colonel Motors models and then settled on a
silver Nossun, rather appropriate for a family with a daughter. He took
me to the dealership for a test drive and approval. I asked him one more
time whether he was happy with a modest car and didn't really want
another Merceles. He assured me that he was happy and grateful and
couldn't wish for anything else.*

## 5

It was Eva's way of reciprocating for the surprise birthday party. I
was thrilled. Though my new car was not a Merceles, it was much
above my current status and I thanked her from the bottom of
my heart. In the grateful mood I impulsively promised to sell the
smoky, foul smelling diesel to the first bidder. Ads went in the
local bargain finder. For sale signs were taped on all windows. A
few prospects responded. The odd prospective buyers took it for a
drive but no offers were made. Finally, one prospect, a mechanic,
asked if he could be frank with me. Then, without waiting for my
consent, he went on to describe a number of things wrong and what
it would cost to fix. He said the car was too dangerous to drive.
However, he would get it towed to his garage if I contributed five
hundred dollars towards essential repairs. He gave me 24 hours to
think it over. Eva was all for accepting his offer. "We will get back
the money from our unused insurance," she pointed out. I had no
honourable way out since I had promised her that I would sell it
to the first bidder. I called him first thing in the morning. Before
I could say yes he said that he had been talking to his colleagues.
The car will really cost much more than he first thought. He now
wanted $750 for my share of the repairs. I had to admit to myself

that the guy was a great negotiator; he knew when he had the other party over a barrel. I did not give him time to think again and hurriedly accepted. That evening I parted with my friend of twenty years and considered the check to the new owner the dowry she deserved for long service.

The new car drives much better, is very quiet, the sound system is wonderful but it is not built like a tank and it does not announce the arrival with great fanfare. Even if it did, I will still miss my faithful old servant like a dear departed friend. I cannot help feeling that a part of me is missing.

# Cabbie

I am Pagal, a cab driver by profession. I rent a cab from my friend Manji, drive it come snow or sun twelve hours a day seven days a week and make a reasonable living. I was not always a cabbie though. I was a geologist back home with the National Oil and Gas Company. I was doing so well that when I married Veena; a big dowry came with her. A couple of years later, her brother Ramji shocked the family. He decided that this five thousand year old culture was not good enough for him and he was going to emigrate to the West. All his mother's entreaties fell on deaf ears. He left a good job at the local University and moved to far off Toronto, a place where, as his mother said, they ate with their left hand and used the same hand to clean themselves with old newspaper rather than fresh water. However, the family felt consoled once he settled there and wrote regularly to them. In addition to the news of his wife Madhu and their two little kids, the letters told tall tales of wonderful life in Canada: no dirt, no dust; turn on the tap, hot water comes out; turn another tap, warm rain cleans all the sweat and dirt off your body; no communal riots; homes and offices cozy all year round; phones that work without a hitch; no blackouts ever; and the clincher - doctors and hospital beds waiting to treat you for free if you get so much as a sniffle.

I wasn't taken in, but Veena was duly impressed and nagged me for days after every letter. For a long time I disregarded her stream of complaints about her life. Then she took matters in her own hands, she refused to sleep with me. She was not going to risk having kids where you had to pay hard earned money to a midwife. I had to give up my evasive ways. I called the Canadian embassy and, after a few attempts, talked to an official who said that they were short of geologists in Canada. She helped us with numerous forms and we were granted immigration papers in a few short months without having to bribe anyone but the security guard. Thanks to my lucky stars, the gentleman came from Veena's village and asked for only half his normal rate. Veena and I considered that a good omen.

A famous astrologer reviewed our horoscopes and chose an auspicious date and time for our departure. We boarded a flight as close to the time as possible. However, several shocks were waiting for us when we moved lock, stock and barrel to Toronto. Ramji had told us only one side of the story. We found that Ramji was not a University Professor as he used to be back home, but worked as a clerk in a small office. He had a large salary when converted to rupees, the lowly currency of the home country, but everything here costs in dollars what it used to cost in rupees there. This meant that they were barely making two ends meet. Four of them lived cooped up in a small apartment where the children had no room to run around. Madhu did all the chores in the house herself because they could not afford even one servant.

Veena was devastated. She had never cooked a meal, leave alone sweep the floor and, heavens forbid, clean the toilet. Now Madhu expected her to pick up with dust pan the food her own kids had dropped on the floor. Helping with the chores frustrated Veena. She told me in no uncertain terms that jet lag or not, I must find a job in a hurry so she could live to the standards she was accustomed. Otherwise, she was going to go back to her mother.

What could be the bigger insult to a proud husband from an upper class family than his wife returning to her mother, particularly after he had spent all her dowry in moving to Toronto? I called an immigration counselor for an appointment. He was booked solid for six months but promised to call me if there was a cancellation.

Veena pointed out with proper indignation that she was not going to be Madhu's servant for six months. She instructed me to look for and find other sources of information. It soon became clear that if I wanted to use my education and experience, we would have to move to Alberta more than two thousand miles away. It was not hard to persuade Veena to do this and Ramji helped us with fares to facilitate the move and found temporary accommodation with Manji, his old school buddy. We moved to Calgary on what the pilot described as the coldest November day on record. The announcement had us shivering till the hostess took pity on us and brought us coffee and crackers. Fortunately, Manji was at the airport to pick us up. He lived in a big house in a suburb and we were given a room to ourselves. A big meal with an unending array of dishes was served. But again, at the end of the meal we were expected to help clean up the mound of utensils. How any self-respecting professional could live without servants was beyond me. When I asked Manji this, he said he was not a professional. He owned a few cars that he let out as taxis to other immigrants from home. They paid him a fixed rent per week, paid for gas and maintenance of the cars and kept whatever was left. The arrangement allowed everybody to make a good living even though drivers had to work twelve hours a day, seven days a week.

I knew from experience back home that to land a good job you needed a resumé prepared by a company of professional job hunters. I found the right company from a spiffy ad in the Yellow pages. They charged me what looked like a fortune when I converted it into rupees. But Veena said it was fine with her if it helped me find a job suitable for my qualifications and we could live comfortably in our own home.

I tore out all the Yellow pages listing oil companies at a phone booth. I circled the companies that looked interesting and started calling them randomly. My spirits were high. I had a postgraduate degree and five years of practical experience in actually finding oil. Moreover, I remembered being told that there was a shortage of geologists. I made it a practice to call a number and ask for the Exploration Manager. Most companies did not have such a post; they hired temporary help when they needed it. Sometimes I was told by the receptionist, rather curtly I thought, that they were reducing staff and I would be wasting time talking to anybody. Other times, kindly men told me that they needed help but only if I had worked before in quaintly named areas like Moose Jaw, Medicine Hat or Red Deer. One frank soul told me that my degrees were useless to him since I knew nothing of local geology and finding oil was a different kettle of fish in Canada than back home.

After a few days of such disappointments I was desperate. I started begging for a start up position; that of a trainee, a junior technician, anything to get a foot in the door. No luck. I soon exhausted the list of oil companies. As the last resort, I looked for the Professional Geologists in Yellow pages, found names that could be from back home and called them. Very few returned my calls. And those who did, repeated the same old thing – need Canadian experience. I asked how I could get this experience without anyone giving me a chance to work. No one gave me an answer to that. They didn't need to. They already had jobs.

Manji took pity on me during one of my spells of acute desperation. One of his drivers had been in hospital for a week. He couldn't drive and was unable to pay the rent. Manji offered to train me for a day and to rent me that cab. I asked him what would happen when the driver came out of the hospital. "Nothing," said Manji. "That guy is history. He will never be able to pay the interest on back rent, leave alone the back rent. I am not going to waste a good cab on that scoundrel," he added. I was sorry for the guy, but I needed a job. I could not return home with my tail between my legs. In any case, there was no job waiting for me there either.

So my twelve hour rounds started. For a while I watched the daily papers for job openings for geologists, whether start up positions or senior executive posts. There was never any acknowledgement of my applications, leave alone the call for an interview. In the end, I gave up thinking of myself as a geologist and became a cabbie. In the meantime, my wife and I rented a small apartment. She was disappointed at having to live in such tiny quarters but happy to have some place to call her own. She even agreed to sleep with me once in a while if I took proper precautions. She got used to doing chores, learnt to cook delicious curries, even got the job of cleaning the hallways and front entrance in our apartment building to help pay the rent. We live frugally, hoping to save enough to buy our own cab one day. Occasionally, we dream of buying Manji's business when his past catches up with him and he is sent to where he belongs. If the dream ever becomes reality, I will still drive a cab to keep my toe in the water, as they say here. But it won't be the long hours and it won't be seven days; I will need time to spend with little ones we will be able to have. Of course, we won't skimp any more, although servants will always be beyond our means and poor Veena will still have to cook and keep the house.

We don't tell all this to the family back home. They won't believe us.

# Lost and Found on a Mountain

1

This is the story of how I lost my way on the Bearpaw Ridge and found my mental peace.

By any measure, my life has been an eventful one. My wife Evelyn and I had lived in four countries on four continents before settling in Canada with our two young daughters, Roshan and Kamini. Anita arrived soon after. I became a reasonably successful consultant in oil industry. Evelyn went to Medical School, opened a very busy practice and acquired an international reputation in Pediatrics. Roshan and Kamini completed postgraduate degrees and started working in their chosen fields. I gave up consulting five years ago and started chasing the rainbow in two venture operations with mixed success. I now had the luxury of spare time when I thought about environmental disasters facing our planet and concluded that six billion people were more than the world could support and this number must be reduced to sustain the diversity of life. To achieve this, I concluded, older people like me who had lived out the useful part of their life should say goodbye to the world and save its limited resources. However, fear of the consequences of failure stopped me from attempts at realizing this idea.

My company has a mineral claim in the dense bush 70 kilometers east of Prince George in British Columbia. The claim is located on Bearpaw Ridge, one kilometer above surrounding valleys. The terrain is very rough and the area is known for grizzlies, black bears and coyotes. There are no trails, but a forestry road circles the ridge. It was here that on a glorious summer morning two days after my sixty-fourth birthday, Brad, our geologist, and I set out to collect soil samples for gold exploration. We were dressed for hard work on a hot day. I wore nylon pants, long sleeved shirt and cardigan, a cotton jacket with mosquito netting for the face and the bald head and a thin nylon jacket. After a tough day of hiking in the dense bush we climbed a cliff to reach the top of the ridge and bagged our last sample at about 5:00 in the evening. It had been an exhausting day and we still had to make our way to the camp.

As I looked down from the top, the descent appeared impossibly steep. But it was nothing to Big Brad who, after safely lodging the last sample in my backpack, raced down the ridge grabbing the branches of pine trees. I could not reach the branches and started making my way down slowly on all fours. I shouted to Brad that I will be slow and will catch up with him down below. I soon lost the sight of Brad. I did not make a special effort to meet up with him because I thought that he interpreted my call to mean that I will meet him at the camp at the base of the ridge. I was not worried about getting lost even though I had no compass, map, food or water. I was certain I will reach the camp before dark. After all, we had a network of data lines tagged extensively. After about half an hour, I did find a line of tags and followed it till it ended against another line at right angles. This line would take me to the logging road near the camp.

Now I made a blunder of the magnitude I do not intend to repeat ever again, if I can help it. I decided to replenish my water supply from a nearby stream I could hear. After some fifteen minutes, I found the stream. However, I never found my way back to the flags. After searching till dark, I decided to spend the first outdoor night in my life next to the stream and use my knowledge of the area to work my way out the next morning. My only thought before falling asleep was that if a bear or a cougar found me, he goes for my neck first. The problem during the night was not wildlife but rain and the stream. The water level in the stream rose during the night and soaked my boots and the backpack. Mosquitoes managed to penetrate the net and inflicted itchy bites. Hard and damp ground and the temperature around freezing were not inducive to a decent sleep.

I was up with daylight at five and decided that heading west will take me to the forestry road where I could hitch a ride. My wet boots squelched at every step and my empty stomach protested. All my backpack contained was twenty pounds of valuable soil samples and a bottle full of cool stream water which I replenished at every opportunity. The clouds were hiding the sun and I did not know which way the west was. I climbed out of the stream channel on to the ridge and followed along the crest hoping that I will come to some familiar point and then make my way out. I passed two sites that looked like abandoned drill holes. Disorientation must have already set in because I thought that they were the holes we had drilled on top of the ridge six years earlier. This was in fact impossible because that is where I had got separated and that area was marked with orange tags every few meters. In the late afternoon, I came to steep slopes on three sides and a vast clear-cut overgrown with intense bush. A stream with muddy banks was straight ahead. If I had followed the stream, I would have reached the road within an hour. But the gods above wanted to test my mettle. I turned left and followed a saddle. The rain was now heavy and the bush wet. Around 7:00 PM I heard someone reciting Sanskrit prayers about saving our souls. I saw a man about 100 meters away swaying on a wheeled trolley while praying. I shouted for help but there was no response. After negotiating a small stream I heard a couple talking. Again, I screamed for help, but to no avail.

It was pouring down buckets now. I found a clump of pine trees and some space which was less damp than the rest. Here I lay down for the night. I resolved that rain, cold, hunger and hallucinations will not gain control over me and slept better this night than before. I shivered quite a lot but shivering was limited to either the top half or the legs. The worst shiver was after I woke up in the middle of the night to pass what felt like a bucket of quite hot water.

Again, I was up with the sun and set off bushwhacking along the slope as much as possible while avoiding muddy areas. After a while, I was out of the clear cut and on a saddle. I followed it for a while till I reached a stream which soon became a swamp with pools of red water. I stayed on the high ground crisscrossing the stream a number of times. As the evening approached, I reached a small clearing and headed for it. As I came out of this clearing, I saw the familiar logging road. I shouted with joy like a mad man. I had hiked in the roughest possible terrain for three days through devil's club and alder bushes, negotiating streams, marsh and huge trunks of dead trees and slept under open skies in freezing cold without any cover. It had rained most of the time and the mosquitoes had given me no respite. I hadn't eaten for three days. Thank goodness I had not come face to face with any wildlife although I had crossed a number of bear tracks. Now the rain had stopped and I had a road to walk on to get to the camp.

But my troubles were far from over. It was 9:15 PM and the camp was ten kilometers away. The probability of a vehicle passing at that time of night was less than zero. Therefore, I started walking at a slow but steady pace. A little while later I saw a helicopter fly by across the valley a few kilometers ahead of me. I realized that cries won't help and I had no energy to waste. As if I hadn't had enough, I discovered with horror that diarrhea had caught up with me. But I kept walking wondering in my confusion how many nights I had been out. I also rehearsed in my mind how I will stop and request a ride to the camp if some vehicle happened to pass by. But none did!

It was nearly midnight when I turned on the logging road to the camp. I was literally at the end of my rope and I still had 5 kilometers of steep walk to get there. However, I had barely walked five minutes when I was blinded by the headlights of some cars coming down the road. I completely forgot the act I had rehearsed over and over and stood on the side to let the cars pass.

## 2

It was Saturday afternoon in Calgary. Evelyn and Anita were heading for the car when the phone rang. It was Evelyn's friend Aisha who was having some problem with her relatives in Nova Scotia. Anita was clamouring to go but Aisha won't let Evelyn get off. Then the second line buzzer went. Fearing a call from the hospital, Evelyn asked Aisha to hold. It was worse than hospital; it was the RCMP from Prince George. They told Evelyn that her husband had separated from Brad on Bearpaw Ridge on Friday afternoon. Brad and the rest of the crew made a thorough search of the area with no success and reported him missing at noon that day. The RCMP was organizing search parties, including a sniffing dog and had a helicopter available to search if the sky was clear. After hearing the officer out, Evelyn asked him whether he was telling her the whole truth and he assured her that he was. Evelyn contacted Kamini in Fredricton, Roshan in Los Angeles and some friends before she and Anita caught the plane for Prince George leaving at 5:00 PM.

Wild thoughts of grizzlies and cougars and narrow crevices, with the only male in the family lying helplessly with broken leg in the wild, were causing a flood of tears around their seats, and they managed to make a big dent in the supply of paper towels on the plane. The RCMP took them to the campsite the next morning. Roshan and Kamini joined them that afternoon. Chris

Bayley from Vancouver, Jim Fossett from Calgary and Evelyn's colleague Bessy Card and her husband who were holidaying in the Kamloops rushed to Prince George to help in the search and to help the family cope with the trauma. Their desperation reached its peak that evening, my third, when it was decided to "postpone" the decision on whether to mount the search again the next day because the temperature was going to drop to below freezing during the night and chances of survival in the bush were becoming minimal. Roshan made a great case for continuing the search but in vain. When the helicopter left for Prince George their last hope was breathing its last. In desperation, Evelyn faced the mountain and hollered, "Nakku, you better come out now, it is your last chance." Anita noted the time; it was 9:15 PM.

There was a buffet dinner set up for the search party and the family was invited to join in. None of them could eat much and Evelyn used the opportunity to thank the volunteers. It was almost midnight when they got their act together and left in a three car caravan for the hotel. Anita was driving the rented SUV in the front, followed by Cards and the RCMP sergeant. Just before they reached the end of the logging road, she pointed out a ghostlike shadow by the roadside. Evelyn thought that it must be some rescuer waiting for the ride. Suddenly they recognized the shadow and Kamini screamed, "It is daddy."


3


I heard the cry as the cars stopped almost running into each other on the gravel road. Evelyn, our three daughters, Bessy and her husband and the RCMP sergeant jumped out of the cars. I was flabbergasted to see my whole family there and asked why they were there and why so much fuss? Without wasting any time to answer a confused man, they had me stripped in no time and put dry clothes on me. I was thankful that the woman taking off my torn and wet pants and underwear was a doctor and not a modest young lady. I was fed a sandwich and a glass of orange juice. Kamini had brought a packet of cashew nuts, my favourite, for just such an occasion and gave it to me. Her incredible optimism in the face of such odds still moves me when I think of it.

Looking at their faces glowing in the dark, I felt the mission of my life fulfilled. I never could imagine that I could provide so much undiluted joy to so many people just by appearing out of he woods. It was the moment of epiphany when I realized that my life meant a lot to them, our lives overlapped and one could not be removed without detracting from the others. Therefore, it was both selfish and foolish to think that I could end my life just because I felt that the useful part of my life was over. The events of the next month confirmed this conclusion.

On Wednesday, the day after we returned home, I felt very well in body and spirit except for my toes. Evelyn and I went to our offices as usual. I spent most of the day giving interviews to the media. The celebrity status was great while it lasted, but I wouldn't wish this kind of celebrity on my worst enemy. Evelyn cancelled a planned visit to a choir workshop. This turned out to be most fortunate as my healthy feeling proved rather short lived. My diarrhea got worse. Stomach cramps became intolerable. I ended up in hospital for three nights. Then the right toe became swollen and had to be operated on to remove the nail. As soon as the right toe was fixed, the left one started playing up. Regular soaking in hot water separated the nail and the pain eventually disappeared. It was the toenail pressing against the skin that was causing swelling and pain. It was exactly a month after the great midnight reunion in the wilderness when I got up without any ache or pain and resumed my morning exercise regimen.

Evelyn was a tower of strength during this challenging period. She loved me, cared for me, got the right medical advice and attention. Anita was most helpful and attentive to whatever contribution she could make. Roshan and Kamini kept in concerned touch. Mutual concern during the crisis brought our family closer together.

Our family received countless phone messages offering help, sympathy cards and e-mail. It is incredible how much anxiety a moment's stupidity by one person can cause among so many people. I probably deserve all I suffered. Still, the suffering was much alleviated when I thought of the kindness and consideration of the family and friends; Jim Fossett, Cards and Chris Bayley who dropped everything and traveled to Prince George, many friends who worried, prayed and hoped for the best and Dolly Fossett who looked after my office with her usual zeal and competence. And of course my partner Shane was there to supply everyone with information about the area and coordinate the search for his friend of 25 years. Scores of strangers volunteered for the joy of the search and rescue effort. My life couldn't be that worthless after all.

This traumatic event reminded me more forcefully than anything ever before that life cannot be taken for granted. I must enjoy the moment; provide for the future but not sacrifice the present; value my family and friends, after all it is they who make it all worthwhile. A niggling doubt still needed resolution. I had thought for a few years that the useful period of my life was over, I was consuming the limited resources of this overcrowded planet, was living because I had no other choice and felt that no one would miss me for long if I disappeared in a stream or marsh. Yet, I endured hard, wet, cold and rough ground for two long lonely nights and during the day walked with great care not to get hurt and conserved energy to survive without food for as long as possible. This inconsistency between belief and action bothered me so much when I was recuperating that I sought the help of a psychologist. He had a simple explanation. A mild depression was behind my "rational thinking" and the urvival instinct was stronger than this depression. My actions were controlled by my subconscious belief – life is precious and must be preserved at all cost. The depth of attachment displayed by my wife, family and friends at the moment of reunion on the dark logging road pulled me out of the depression. Now I must make the most of this life. No more thought of wasting resources, only of how to return more than I am taking.

# Two Letters

## 1. Father to son

Dearest Chatney:

It has been some weeks since we heard from you. Your mother and sisters are getting worried about you. We hear of extreme cold weather in February in Canada and all that white stuff falling from the sky. Your mother has brought you up to be careful and we are not worried about you going out in cold without long johns, boots, hat and top coat. We are worried about you being a hot-blooded young man though. Funny thoughts enter young heads in cold nights. With all these western girls running after wonderful young Indian men brought up in good families, you will understand why your mother sheds buckets of tears every morning after having nightmares about you and some girl in a miniskirt or less succeeding in trapping you for good.

Personally, I am broad minded, as you know. I will have no objection to you marrying a good girl from family comparable to ours. Operative terms being offered here by comparable families are good. I will be very unhappy if you marry some cheapskate dressed and made up like a Bollywood extra who looks at you as a ticket for the good life till she divorces you, *Hai Bhagwan*, for someone more to her sinful liking. To prevent such a possibility, I insist that you make your home here in India, even if you want to live separately from your parents. Your mother's heart will of course be broken when you give up all these sweet young things waiting for you here with big dowries, but she will console herself if she is able to see you once or twice a day and by thinking of fair-complexioned grandchildren, which you will have many of, no doubt. I can't do much to stop you if you stay there except to say that such an action on your part will make finding husbands for your sisters impossible without the promise of dowries big enough to wipe us out completely.

Gulam visited us the other day and made things worse for your mother and sisters. You remember Gulam. He lived next door when we lived in that little bungalow on Nehru Road. He spent every afternoon at our place asking your mother for just one more samosa. He knows somebody who spent a month in Toronto on some kind of scholarship. This friend told him that girls there wear very tight pants and sweaters and leave nothing to the imagination. When it is even slightly warm, they come out in such tiny skirts; girls here will die of shame just looking at them. Shame, says Gulam, the girls there have none. They hop into bed with anybody who buys them a drink or pays for their food. Most couples are not married, but they have children like married people. What is more, women go out to work, leaving their little ones with strangers who have no idea how to look after children. When women come home, they expect their men to have the house clean and dinner ready. And dinner they expect is not just curry and rice. Oh no. It must be some kind of soup, followed by some meat, potatoes and green vegetables cooked Western style and then dessert of some cake or pastry and coffee with no milk or sugar. How can anyone drink black coffee without sugar? Just the thought makes me sick.

Gulam says that men are slaves of women there. They call it Woman's Lip or something like that. Your sisters do not mind this but your Momma says that if their men were real men, they will keep women where they belong. But much worse, the thought of you having meat, leave alone cooking it, is enough to make every one throw up. We can't even think of you stooping so low. No good girl from a good family will ask you to give up your religion. Of course we know you will have nothing to do with girls who will agree to go out with men without someone from their family accompanying them. You have to think of their reputation, as much as your own.

We don't know all these tales we hear, how much is true and how much imagination of people with nothing worthwhile to do. We are sure though, that our son knows right from wrong just as he knows right from left. He also knows what he owes his Momma and Pappa who have looked at him all through his childhood as the only precious thing they possessed. Remember when you were ten and caught pneumonia. The circle of sadhus that surrounded your bed 24 hours a day for seven days saying prayers in Sanskrit which no one could understand but which worked. Not only you recovered, you took the exam the following week and passed, though barely. Your Momma is thinking of arranging similar prayer gathering around a full size picture of you to protect you from harm on other side of the world.

I am going on and on, as if all the stories we are told are true and even if they are true as if you have fallen victim to some wicked western woman. There have to be good people there, just as there are bad people here. You have enough sense to identify good people to befriend, otherwise you wouldn't have got the scholarship. On this score, I will offer you one word of advice before I shut up. A good girl will want to live in India and bring up her children away from the sinful ways of the West and under the guidance of her in-laws. If she doesn't agree, nay suggest it herself, she is not worthy of you and your family. Surely you don't need reminding that we can give up dowry, but we can't give up the good name of family. If our name is dust, no dowry will help me find homes for your

169

sisters. And you and your bossy wife will not like them to move over to live with you in Sinland, will you?

Enough is enough. I always believed that my son will ask for advice when he needs it. He hasn't asked so he doesn't need any. We have brought him up to bring lustre to family name and no sinful woman can change that.

Your proud Pappa

## 2. Mother to daughter

Dear Sabzi:

It has been a while since I heard from you, three whole days. No doubt, the children are playing up again and their father is working so hard he doesn't have time for them or you. Must pay the mortgage, credit card bills are mounting, utilities keep going up, cars need urgent repairs, roof is leaking, kids need new clothes for winter and on and on he goes, and you agree. Well, let me tell you. If you let him off from his share of housekeeping under these pretexts, you are signing a bond of slavery for life. Soon there will be new demands like school books and then college fees, grocery bill will steadily go up, cars will get older; I could go on but I won't. Suffice to say that there will be enough reasons to stay away from doing the dishes, taking kids to playground, helping with the laundry as long as there is a slave to do it.

It is time you took control of the situation otherwise you will never have time to talk to your own dear Momma, let alone any other source of empathy that a young mother needs from time to time. Take it from your Momma that you have to train a man, even if he is a fine man like your Pappa always was, into being a good husband. Good husbands are not born like good wives are; they are trained. It is a sorry state that mothers don't take this aspect of their sons' future life seriously and the responsibility of training falls on the shoulder of young wives. It is doubly unfortunate because the best time for training is soon after marriage but women are blinded by love and are too ready to excuse their men for transgressions which become more and more bothersome with passage of time and really cumbersome with additions to the family.

Before you ask me to shut up and mind my own business, I will tell you some essentials in training of a husband. I have to tell you this because no mother wants her daughter to be a slave, no matter how good a husband is. Actually, to be a good husband, a man must be considerate. Unfortunately, men of your generation were not brought up to think of any one but themselves. So, it falls on women to teach them the basics of decency; for their sake as much as for a balanced family life. Believe me, dear Sabzi, running around picking dirty underwear is no fun for long, howsoever good a husband is in bed.

Thankfully, training husbands is not as hard as you may think. Men, at least the ones brought up by good mothers, respect women, nay are afraid of women, even if they manage to hide their fears most of the time. Recognition of this basic trait of men is the first step towards liberation of young women from slavery. Once you firmly believe that men listen, even when they pretend to be deaf, you are halfway there. However, if you have any doubts, these are conveyed to your prey and he becomes slippery. Therefore, get rid of any doubt in your ability to bring to the fore the fear your husband has of you as a woman.

Once you have won this battle with yourself, the road is clear. All you need to do is: issue clear instructions. Vagueness won't do. For heaven's sake don't say, "Come home around six." Be specific and say, "Be home by six." If he is late, even by a few minutes, ask what held him up. Don't wait for him to tell you. You will wait for ever and you will be the one waiting trying to keep dinner hot every evening for the rest of your life. Even if he has a good reason, and heavy traffic is not a good reason, look irritated and be mad with the kids. Remember how I used to be mad with your brother for no reason when Dad was late. Now you know why. It worked every time with him, remember. It will work for you too. It has worked in every generation since Eve. And I am not talking of your aunt Eve.

If it is a one time request, state the time frame. Just saying, "Dear, the tap in bathroom is leaking" will never work. Remember men are slippery like eels. For you to get the tap fixed you will have to say, "Darling, the tap in the bathroom has been leaking for days. Can you fix it before the weekend?" I will bet your Pappa's RRSP, if you are that specific, the tap will not be leaking by the weekend. If it is, you have to ask him why, and show your disappointment in no uncertain terms.

The key, and there is only one so you don't even need a key ring, is to be firm, give just enough wiggle room to leave a sense of freedom, and be ready to punish. If you are not going to punish, it won't work. If you fix the tap yourself, I can guarantee you that he will make certain you eventually end up doing the job you assigned him. To set him on the right course, call the most expensive plumber in town at a time when the husband is there and put the bill on his card. It seems expensive but it really is not. That is because you will have to do it only once. Next time there is need for a repair, it will be done well before the deadline you set.

Please Sabzi, take your dear Momma's advice. Set a curfew time for him to be home. Start assigning him duties which any respectable husband should be happy to take over. Start taking time off from home and hearth for R & R before you are so stressed that your Momma has to come over for weeks to look after your family and set your husband straight.

I will leave you now with these thoughts. Call or write to me soon. A mother needs her daughter's love as much as the daughter needs her mother's wisdom.

Your doting Momma.

# A Memorable Journey

1

I am a short invisible sort of guy who came to Canada from India to eke out a living on the oil patch. Mehdi is a tall imposing man. He came to North America from Egypt in his twenties to do a doctorate in Geology, joined a major oil company in Canada on graduation, married a petite blonde and settled into the life of a successful professional. In due course he set up his own consulting business. He needed some help in my specialty. That is how we started working together and ended making a business trip to Katara.

Our long flight from Calgary to Nicetown, the capital of Katara, included a welcome overnight break in Big Bang. In anticipation of landing a big contract, both of us were in a celebratory mood when we boarded the flight. I asked the hostess on the plane for my usual white wine, medium dry if possible, please. After ordering dry red for himself, Mehdi turned to me and asked in a suitably deprecatory tone,

"You don't know much about wines, do you?"

"No, I don't know anything. You know we Hindus are not allowed alcohol. So my drinking is limited to the occasions when my wife is not looking," I timidly replied.

"We Muslims are not allowed either. But when in Rome do as the Romans do. So, I worked hard to cultivate Western tastes.

People with refined taste only drink red," he condescendingly advised me. As if to complete my education he added, "And Hindus don't eat beef either. So you have your steak well-done. I should tell you that steak is eaten rare, with blood dripping from red meat, not after the juices have escaped through the chimney."

It was too late to change my order. Over his refined red and my uncivilized white, we discussed our plans for the evening in Big Bang. It transpired that it was his fiftieth birthday that day and a big party was planned on his return when all kinds of alcohol would flow down the cultivated Muslim throats from fine Venetian glasses. I took all my courage in both hands and asked if we should celebrate his birthday by going to some fine dining room. He agreed, so long as he selected the wine and I ordered my steak rare.

After checking in a five star hotel appropriate for his station but way beyond my means, we refreshed ourselves with a relaxing hot shower, probably the last for the next two weeks, and met in the dining room at six. The beautiful room on the top floor of the hotel had a great view of the harbour. After a dry sherry as the starter, we ordered the steaks and he ordered a bottle of French wine, red of course. In short order, the young and obviously inexperienced waiter opened the bottle and presented the cork to Mehdi. He delicately picked it and held it about a foot from his face to let the aroma drift to his nose. The reaction showed me that things were not as they should be but the waiter did not notice as he was totally absorbed in pouring wine for tasting. Mehdi picked up the glass, stirred the wine by shaking glass anti-clockwise, held it at some distance to examine the bouquet and reluctantly took a sip. He should have followed his instinct and not gone to that extreme. The sip almost choked him on its way down his throat and he quickly drank a whole glass of water. "Take it away, take it away, cork was not airtight," he screamed. The poor waiter didn't know what to do. So he brought the head waiter to the table. This gentleman ordered his underling to bring him a glass so he could determine himself how bad the wine really was. After ceremoniously pouring into the glass, shaking it and sipping the wine, he agreed, without choking, that Mehdi was right and the wine had gone off. Since bad cork was a random problem, not likely to repeat itself, Mehdi instructed him to bring another bottle of the same.

The whole process of ceremonious opening, cork sniffing, wine pouring, wine sniffing and tasting was repeated. But this time the lingering frown was replaced by a smile and the waiter was ordered to pour both glasses, which he did. However, no sooner had he done that, the headwaiter returned with a message Mehdi was wanted on the phone. He went to the phone and returned in a few seconds. "I got to run; some one needs to see me," he said on his way to the door. "Just carry on and don't wait for me."

He disappeared and I was left alone to celebrate his birthday. It took me several hours to drink the whole bottle of foul-tasting red wine by myself and push past my unwilling taste buds the uncooked beef. When I finished, it was almost midnight and I didn't know which window overlooked the harbour. I paid the bill bloated by various taxes and miscellaneous charges and somehow found my room. I was too uncultivated for Mehdi to ever tell me who he had to meet. I didn't ask because it was none of my business. I am sure the petite blonde arranging the birthday party never found out either. She is still with him.

## 2

Our ten hour drive to Oilcity, a small city in the northeast corner of Katara, was uneventful except for dusty roads with more potholes than asphalt. We stayed in the best hotel in town where hot coffee was a spoonful of instant coffee in a cup and an open jug of lukewarm water and the poached egg needed a chisel and hammer to cut through it. Our meetings were pleasant affairs with a lot of nodding in agreement to comments made in a language the other party couldn't properly understand. On our last evening, we were invited by the hosts to a dinner in the local restaurant famous all over the region for its native cuisine. The location on a street with stagnant pools of dirty water and chickens and pigs roaming freely left something to be desired, but the inside was clean and decorated with beautiful Kataran statuettes.

After numerous toasts to the friendship between our countries, our companies, our families and us individually, the food started arriving. Mehdi enjoyed the forbidden pork and I relished well-done beef. Then came the high point of the dinner, a delicacy prepared especially for the distinguished guests from Canada. It was brought in a huge tray covered with a lid and placed ceremoniously in front of Mehdi. When the owner of the restaurant removed the lid Mehdi did a wonderful job of hiding his shock, a feat I couldn't copy. Luckily, all eyes were on the tray adorned with a whole chicken, wings, feathers, beaks, eyes and all, cooked to perfection on low heat for ten hours, we were told. Our hosts asked Mehdi to do the honour of pulling the beak out and sucking it. I don't know how he managed to do it, I was sick to my stomach and only the poor lighting hid my state from the hosts. Maybe it did not. The next morning we were told that our services were not what they needed then and they would contact us when their need arose.

3

Things have improved there since that trip to Katara and I now look back on my experience on the return trip with some amusement. But it could have been my last trip to anywhere.

We returned to Nicetown with bruised egos and shaken bodies. Mehdi was joining a tourist group for another week, so I was on my own on the return trip. While checking the time of my return flight to Big Bang, I discovered that my reservation had been cancelled because I had not confirmed it on arrival in Katara. The next available flight was in two months, a little late for my connecting flights to Vancouver. After some thrashing about, I found the last seat in the business class on a plane leaving in the afternoon for Lucky Bay, an industrial town on the mainland across a narrow channel from Big Bang. Once there, I could cross the channel on a short foot-bridge and take a cab to the airport. This was the plan.

I got to Nicetown airport in good time. A taciturn ticket clerk closely inspected my passport, visa, credit card and driving license and issued the boarding pass. It was in Katarese and all Greek to me. On my way to the boarding gate, a security guard checked the boarding pass and the passport and made sure that I was the rightful owner of both. I boarded the plane, put my briefcase in the overhead bin and sat down in my aisle seat anticipating the pleasant company of the young lady in the window seat. Much to my dismay, she got up instantly, called the hostess and started an intense discussion in Katarese. I sat wondering whether I had forgotten to use deodorant after the shower or worse. Perhaps the lady had noticed my Indian origin and my presence revived painful memories of a close relative lost in Indo-Katarese conflicts of a generation ago.

My fears were groundless. At the end of their conversation, the hostess asked me if I would mind changing my seat with the young lady's boyfriend in the first class. I readily accepted, knowing that washrooms in the first class had toilet paper, a luxury not supplied in business class. Incidentally, the wash rooms in tourist class were used for stacking cargo, not for the passengers' convenience.

In a few minutes an elderly gentleman with the smile of a sugar daddy exchanged his boarding pass with me and I walked up to my new seat. The plane started slowly, then picked up speed, only to lose it just before takeoff and came to a grinding halt. We sat there for an hour in the sweltering heat, twiddling our thumbs. Then the pilot announced that the plane had engine trouble and returned to the boarding gate. We got off the plane and, after a couple of hours of suffocation in a small waiting room, were bused to a hotel down town. There was no information on when the plane would be ready to leave, whether in a few hours or in a few days. The good news was that the hotel had rooms for the next few days if we had the money to pay in advance.

Just as we sat down to order dinner, the airline's messengers started herding the passengers back on the buses. The plane was ready! Half way to the airport, a jolt interrupted my enjoyment of the countryside and the jolt was not due to the bus hitting a speed bump at full speed. It was the realization that the boarding pass peeping out of my pocket was not mine. What would the security guard do when he notices this?

Horrible visions of the rest of my life spent in a prison started dancing on the bald pate of the man in the seat ahead of me. It would be unwise for the Canadian embassy to risk relations with an important trading partner whose cheap exports were keeping inflation down in Canada by defending an immigrant of Indian origin, and the Indian government would not fight for a renegade who had given up the citizenship of that great nation for a western country with a smaller population than the smallest state in India. I also remembered reading that prisoners in Katara of those days had to be fed by their families or they had to buy food from prison guards at black market rates. Since my funds were rather limited, I consoled myself that, one way or the other, the misery of prison life was unlikely to last long for me. Starvation would bring me salvation.

This frightening train of thought made the journey to the airport seem endless. Before I had time to return to he present, we were lining up at the security desk. Not knowing any of the numerous local dialects, I had no way other than to look and act the innocent fool. So I presented the boarding pass and the passport while examining the dust particles on my shoes. Miracle of miracles, the guard examined the papers and waved me on! It must have been heavenly intervention on behalf of an atheist, for I do not remember folding a hundred dollar bill in my passport.

I got to Lucky Bay at midnight and found a hotel. I called my wife and left a short message. The message got garbled on its long journey of a few milliseconds and she imagined her diminutive husband, with a suitcase poised shakily on his head, wading across the shoulder deep waters of the channel separating mainland Katara from Big Bang. In truth, the bridge crossing was a piece of home-baked pecan pie topped with whipped cream compared to the events of the previous day. I took a cab to the airport, checked in for the flight and made my way to the Maple Leaf Lounge. There, as I reclined on the sofa with recent editions of *Globe and Mail*, a glass of wine, white of course, and a bowl full of nuts, I experienced what it must be like to be in heaven, even for a disbeliever like me.

Who said I won't go to Katara again for a million dollars?

# Isolde's Dream

## 1

"Yes mama. I will engage Herr Mahler. He will find the best singer, select the orchestra, and conduct a performance that will be a tribute to your memory. The world will come to the performance and the songs will be played all over the world. They will be called Wesendonck Lieder. Yes mama, after the premiere, they will be sung in every music room in Germany. Every young woman will dream the "Dream" when singing "Liebestod". Mama, Mathilde Wesendonck will live as long as Richard Wagner lives."

"Myrrha, the love of Mathilde and Richard lives with these songs. Love is the foundation of Art. If love dies, Art will perish with it. Without Art, there will be no mankind."

"Mama, you are sounding more and more like Herr Wagner used to. Everybody is talking like him, even thinking like him. I don't understand this fascination. Do you?

"Dear, one day you will. One day every one will. Great Art is like great wine. You need the right ingredients, careful handling and correct aging. To appreciate great wine, you need to cultivate great taste. It all takes time. Trouble too. Once you develop the taste, your life changes, for the better. Go now. I am ready to dream, dream of my love, of my life that was not to be."

☉☉

One fine summer afternoon, on my way home from the bookstore, I noticed a magnificent carriage leave the gate. Our home was not a palace like many in Düsseldorf, but it was spacious and comfortable. Our carriage was functional and got us to the shops and parties without attracting any attention. Our staff wore presentable uniforms, but nothing elegant. Once in a while, Papa liked to entertain small groups. Large balls were not our style. We spent our evenings reading, playing music and play acting. I wrote small childish plays for our family to perform on these evenings and when, carried away by fancy, I wrote poems, these were carefully hidden from every one.

There was excitement in the air when I entered the drawing room where Mama and Papa were talking merrily. As soon as I entered, they got up and both tried to hug me at the same time. I was thoroughly confused. "Mama, please, what is the excitement about? Has a publisher accepted my plays?" I asked. Both replied at the same time, "No, no. It is much greater, much more exciting. Sit down. We want our Mathilde comfortable when she hears this."

The suspense was killing me. What can be greater than my plays being published? Mama could not hold it any longer, "Oh dear. The Wesendoncks want to join our family. Wesendoncks, the silk merchants. Their son Otto is smitten by you and wants to marry you."

"Mama, I am barely eighteen. I don't want to marry and be a hausfrau for another ten years. Please Papa, do I have a say in what happens to me?"

"Of course you have dear." They both replied in unison. Mama carried on, "As for being only eighteen, I was sixteen when I married Papa and a good thing I did. No better man ever existed, as you well know. Of course, we cannot commit you to marry, least of all to some one you have never met. So we two are invited to stay with them in Berlin for a month when it is convenient for you. It will give you and Otto time to know each other and you to make up your mind whether you are ready to marry Otto."

Papa sent a letter to the Wesendoncks setting our departure in six weeks. The time went by quickly. Three tailors and their assistants were kept busy making cozy travel garments, fancy petticoats and new dresses for Mama and me. Papa bought blue silk with gold embroidery which had recently arrived from India and Mama designed for me a dress cut low to display the cleavage with great effect. New shoes and hats were ordered and were delivered only two days before we left. The packing was finished barely an hour before the coach was due to leave.

Mama and I were received at the station by a handsome young couple, Otto and his sister Myrrha. Both bowed deeply to Mama and expressed gratitude at the opportunity of playing host to us. Myrrha greeted me with great affection and Otto held my hand when I offered it to him just a little bit too long. He had trouble taking his eyes off me and I returned the compliment in my own shy manner. A magnificent carriage pulled by four white horses carried us to a large estate several kilometers away from the city. The footman opened the gate and we had a view of the well-tended English-style garden in front of a broad stone building. As the carriage stopped the middle-aged Wesendonck couple came out to greet us. We were led into a small chamber overlooking an apple orchard. Coffee and cakes were served to tide us over until dinner. Our hosts were solicitous about the exhausting 500 kilometer long journey by mail coach and remarked how well we looked in spite of it. When I had finished my coffee, Herr Wesendonck suggested that the young people go on a short walk while our luggage was being unpacked by the maids.

The kindness of this unpretentious family and Otto's consideration for my slightest wish was flattering. But it was the maturity of Otto and his concern for my future welfare, both physical and intellectual, that won me over. A few months later, the uneventful childhood of a pretty girl in a comfortable family in Düsseldorf changed at the age of nineteen. My world of books, music, plays and art came to an abrupt end as I was married to Otto, scion of the famous Wesendonck family who traded silk from India and China to Europe and America.

Otto was a mature thirty and helped me settle into a life of luxury I could not have even dreamed of. It didn't take long before our first baby decided to arrive. We named her after her aunt Myrrha. Soon after her arrival we moved to New York for Otto to take charge of that end of the business.

Life in New York was a series of balls, with frequent travel to Boston, Philadelphia and Chicago. It was amusing to watch the pretensions of these small towns as if they were the centre of the universe. Still, even a young woman like me could see that the future was here. Otto was occupied in setting up the American foundations of his business empire for three years. We added baby Guido to the family. I returned to writing in my spare time and managed to write some poems and a play which Otto was pleased to read. Then, as suddenly as it had started, our stay in the new world came to an end.

Otto received word that he was needed in Switzerland. Otto was excited about the move but it didn't matter to me. I was as happy in New York with my Otto, my Myrrha and baby Guido as I would be in Zurich. Myrrha was ready to walk and it was exciting to see her standing up and trying to lift her right foot without falling over. Guido was a happy baby and we were lucky to have a competent nurse for him. We were not pleased with our other staff in New York. The Americans never learnt how to serve and, believe me, they wanted to be paid as much as Otto was earning.

Within three short months we had moved to a rented villa in Zurich. I was excited about the villa Otto was going to build for us. He had already signed the deal to acquire the land and engaged the architect. It was a beautiful property overlooking the Zurichsee and the villa was to sit on a small hill with a clear view of sunrise and sunset. I had instructed the architect to build a music room large enough to have an audience of twenty for performances by an octet. The music room should stand by itself separate from the villa to preserve the calm needed by the artists to bring out their best.

Between the children and the planning of the villa, it did not leave much time for parties, yet it was good for Otto to accept some invitations. It helped to bring him out of his shell and he enjoyed telling his equals what was wrong with Europe and what to do about it. The more he drank, the more was wrong and the more complex his solutions became.


## 3


Otto came home very excited one evening. We were invited to meet Herr Wagner at a dinner by Herr Marschall, our lawyer. Madame Wille, who was our neighbour and had introduced us to Zurich society, had mentioned him to us. She had admired his operas in Dresden had told us that he was a member of the group that had tried to overthrow the king of Saxony and was now sheltering in Zurich. Otto and I had never met a revolutionary before. Otto was looking forward to locking horns with him and I was eager to enjoy the battle of the two titans. On the appointed day, I dressed with greater care than I exercised for dinners hosted by Otto's underlings. Not flashy, mind you, but immaculate in style with matching jewelry.

The Marschalls lived in a modest home in a part of Zurich that was once fashionable. It soon became obvious that they had gone to extraordinary lengths to host the dinner. Six couples were already there when we arrived. As usual, the ladies were exchanging local gossip on one side of fireplace and the gentlemen were discussing politics on the other. Discussing is not quite the word. They all seemed to be expressing their opinions on whatever subject they were talking about to one person standing in the centre of the group. As soon as we were announced, Herr and Frau Marschall hurried to the door and, after initial formalities, took us both to the male group.

Herr Marschall introduced the man in the centre to us. He was the revolutionary we had come to meet. Indeed, Herr Wagner did not look like a revolutionary at all. He was barely five feet six inches tall and very gaunt, as if he had been starving. He was immaculately dressed in an elegant silk shirt and slightly lose dinner jacket which was frayed around the collar. His head was the shape of an inverted pear, black shiny hair making his head even bigger than it was. The only attractive features were his penetrating dark blue eyes and the general demeanour that commanded attention and respect. He bowed to Otto and kissed the hand I offered him. "Madam Wille has told us about the successes of your operas in Dresden and your great performances of Beethoven's Ninth which is a poet's work which can only be presented by another poet," I said when he straightened up.

He appeared pleased by these comments and, spoke in a sing song style, "I am delighted to meet such a charming couple I have heard so much of. I do hope that I will get to know you better."

"How long do you expect to favour us with your presence in Zurich," I asked.

He bowed deeply, "The decision is not mine to make, since German authorities do not want me back in Germany out of a misunderstanding on their part."

It was Otto's turn to ask, "Herr Wagner, can you throw more light on the reasons of misunderstanding?"

"Other than stating that the reasons are political, I will rather not delve into the subject. I am an artist and to serve the German people through art is the sole purpose in my life. I want to build on

Beethoven and Weber and combine music with poetry, drama, ballet and architecture to present opera as a total work of art, as was done in glory days of ancient Greece. To achieve these ends, Germans have to remove from existing art in Germany all evil French and Italian influences and create what is in the soul of 'German *volk*'."

Just as he was about to take off on this flight of fancy, he saw a piano in the far corner. It was an old-style grand piano of an unfamiliar make. "Excuse me," he said to no one in particular, "I must try my aging fingers on Frau Marschall's instrument." In a moment he had raised the lid and was sitting on the piano stool stretching his fingers. He checked the tuning, smiled and asked the hostess, "How much time do we have before the dinner is served?"

Frau Marschall, delighted at the turn of events, replied, "Herr Wagner, will half an hour be enough time for you?"

He nodded and looked up to the heavens through the ceiling as if for inspiration. All eyes turned to him. He said in hushed tones as if awed by what he was going to play, "Ladies and gentlemen, the last movement of Beethoven's Ninth as transcribed for piano by my friend, the great pianist Franz Liszt." Before his fingers hit the piano our eyes met and I sensed a hunger for love in them.

It soon became clear that piano was not his forte, yet every one there was mesmerized. It was his feeling for the music, as if the composer lived in him. The tempos were different than I remembered, sometimes a little slower, sometimes a little quicker. I could hear Schiller's words through the music even though I only vaguely remembered them. The glow on his face became brighter as the music proceeded. And, as if in no time, the playing was over. His fingers still resting on the last keys, he slumped forward. Everyone felt the thrill of being touched by something unique and uplifting. Applause and bravos broke the spell. He gathered himself together, looked at me once more and I felt close to him, so close that I was scared. A married woman does not feel one with a stranger without dangerous repercussions.

Dinner was very pleasant but uneventful. Herr Wagner was at the other end of the table and was barely heard from, as if the piano had sucked all energy out of him. There was discussion about German unification and the political situation in Europe. Otto was very clear that Germans were too fractious to ever unite and the French republic was a farce and would be short-lived. The discomfort of our main guest was there for all to see but he did not participate in the discussions. When the hostess asked him to comment, he mumbled that he was merely a struggling artist, in no position to comment on weighty matters like these.

After dinner and a short break for men to smoke their cigars, all the ladies insisted that Herr Wagner play some of his own music. It did not take much persuasion for him to return to the piano. After some light pieces from his early works which sounded like Bellini and Weber, he settled down to play the sketches from his recent operas. There was the spinning song from *The Flying Dutchman*, the Pilgims' chorus from *Tannhauser*, and the wedding march from *Lohengrin*. Everyone was mesmerized and wanted more. Just before taking our leave, Otto, businessman that he was, proposed to Herr Wagner the sponsorship of two concerts during the winter. Herr Wagner accepted, so long as he had complete freedom to select the artists and the program. They settled on a date and time to meet to discuss the details. Otto asked Herr Wagner if he would mind my presence, "She is the artist in the family." Herr Wagner looked thrilled and suggested that my views on programming would be very useful to him.

4

On the appointed day, precisely on time, Herr Wagner was announced. He was dressed smartly. His suit showed its age but was freshly ironed, shoes well- polished. Otto and I met him in the morning room. He graciously accepted coffee and asked me if I would be happy with Beethoven and Wagner, or did I have other suggestions. I proposed Beethoven's seventh symphony as a good introduction to his own music. He face lit up at the suggestion and he said excitedly that this showed my appreciation of his music more than anything I could have said. It was decided that the first concert would open with this piece and end with selections from *Rienzi, Lohengrin and Tannhauser*. The second concert would open with the Prelude to *Lohengrin*, include selections from *The Flying Dutchman* and his early unperformed operas and end with Beethoven's ninth symphony.

Otto was quite pleased with our rapid agreement. To my total surprise, he announced that he had learned of the tight financial circumstances Herr Wagner found himself in. Otto offered to help Herr Wagner if he was allowed to do so. Herr Wagner expressed his delight and suggested a meeting in a few days when he would make a proposal to the advantage of both sides.

Herr Wagner started visiting us, rather me, because Otto was usually out on business, almost every week. His excuse was that we needed to discuss the artists for the orchestra, although my ignorance about individual artists should have been obvious to him. I did help as a conduit between him and Otto on the cost commitments. If Otto was alarmed by the high rates the artists were to be paid, he did not show it. One morning, Herr Wagner came in with a bulging folder and asked me if I would like to hear him read one of his stories. I readily consented.

This was the story he had written fifteen years earlier when he and his wife lived in penury in Paris. The story described the hardships an artist named R suffered because he would not compromise his artistic vision. His futurist compositions were rejected unseen by the impresarios and he was reduced to write on starvation wage supplementary music for the artistically poor works of popular composers. The humiliations suffered by R moved me to tears and when he read about R's missing pet dog running away when it happened to cross paths with its old master, my tears became a flood. "You are the R of the story. You were writing about yourself, weren't you?" I asked in between the sobs.

His eyes became misty too as he took my hands in both his. He did not need to say a word, his eyes told me all. I was moved as never before, "As long as I live, an artist with the talent like yours will not suffer deprivation again," the words came from my heart.

"I will not let such a kind person as you down. With your support, my art will restore German honour and bring greatness to the stage the world has not seen since ancient Greece," he replied.

We agreed that from then on I would address him as R when we were not in public. He asked me whether I had any artistic aspirations. I said that I had written a few stories and short plays to while away the time but nothing to be proud of. He requested me to dig them out and to read them to him on his next visit.

I was nervous the next time R visited. I decided to read him a play about a young girl in love with her tutor I had written seven years earlier without quite finishing it. He heard it with rapt attention without interrupting me once. When I had finished he sat still for a while collecting his thoughts. When he spoke it was in a gentle tone. He complimented me on my command of language, my skill to express emotions and the ingenuity at vital points in a plot which could quite easily become commonplace. But the play lacked drama, he said. I needed to surprise the reader, even to shock him. For a teenage girl, it was a very commendable effort, he added and hoped that I would finish the play and continue writing. Then he asked me to read to him any poetry I may have written. I promised to do that after he had read to us on his next visit what he was currently writing.

R did not show up for weeks. When he did come, he looked haggard and in need of food and sleep. He told me that his wife had joined him at last and his apartment, which was quite comfortable

190

for him alone, was cramped with his wife and her sister. He had not been sleeping well, his work had come to a halt, and his eczema had flared up again. After feeding him his favourite sauerkraut and hot milk I promised to discuss with Otto if he could help secure better accommodation. He expressed appreciation for my kindness, thanked me for the refreshments and left. He looked relaxed now and the back of his neck was no longer red. I was able to send him a message the next day that Otto had rented for them a more comfortable apartment where they could move next week and that Otto would charge only a nominal rent as long as Herr Wagner made satisfactory progress with his writing.

He was over as soon he received the message. He apologized that Minna, his wife, could not join him in thanking us for our great generosity. He felt proud that we appreciated his art and confident that he would repay our favours through the greatness of his music dramas. He assured us that his new works would change the way Germans viewed opera, and music would never be the same. He rushed to the piano and played a few notes. He said that was how the opera he was working on would open. The notes sounded strange but not unpleasant. Otto remarked that he could see a new direction being set for music and he felt honoured to contribute to it in his own humble way. He promised to try to be present whenever Herr Wagner wished to share his works with us. R was pleased and promised to show us the outline of his drama that would be the greatest work of stage the world has seen.

5

R had some milk before opening the folder he had brought. This was the story line already set in poetry for his new music drama *Siegfried's Tod*, the Death of Siegfried. It was based on the ancient stories of *Edda* and *Niebelungenlied*. He said that he intended this to be one grand opera but after completion became convinced that the work could not be understood on its own. He expressed the desire to read the poem to us. All he asked in return was our honest opinion of his work, particularly places where the audience would have difficulty following the story. He then sang to us in a pleasant baritone the prologue which set the scene for the drama. Three Norns were weaving the thread of fate and telling the story of the beginning of the world when the god Wotan came, drank from the spring and made a staff for his spear from the ash tree. Wotan wrote all the treaties he entered into on the staff. Over time the spring dried and the ash tree withered away. Then suddenly the thread of fate broke predicting the end of the world of god Wotan.

We were absolutely thrilled by the singing as he changed his voice from one Norn to the other and modulated his voice for maximum impact. When the thread broke, he conveyed the shock by the voice and gestures and we both felt the earth quake. He gave us time to fully recover before saying that he would be back with more. He collected his papers, thanked us for the hospitality and was gone. We were shaken to the core by the experience and sat there looking at the chair occupied by him, unable to say a word.

R's morning visits became a weekly affair again. He read, rather sang, the continuation of *Siegfried's Tod*. But when Otto was away, he insisted on listening to my creations. He unfailingly complimented me on good points and politely suggested what could be improved. I always felt encouraged by his criticism and he said in so many words that I had talent which could blossom with work. There were days when I felt ethereal because a genius had admired my work. Otto could see that and was glad I was so happy. He had another reason to be glad. I was more responsive to his needs that he was too civilized to force on me and obliged him more frequently than ever before. I was starting to enjoy it myself.

Time started to take wings as we got into his "poem" as he called it. He got me to start work on a play. Before long we were alternating on readings of our works. I was always flattered when he asked for my opinion. He was very anxious that what he wrote would be clear to the audience and once in a while I was able to point out some vagueness. He always vehemently defended his draft, but on his next visit he would show me the change he had made and asked if the clarity had improved. Similarly, he was quick to point out confused thought or writing in my work but left it to me to work out improvements rather than suggest them to me. Once I asked for suggestions, he declined on the grounds that an art work must be the creation of one person. She alone is in contact with the real creator of that work.

R's visits became infrequent. He said he was trying to complete the poem as soon as possible. He dropped by when he felt tired and needed a change. One such evening he announced that the work was almost complete and he would, if we wished, read it to Otto and me. We set a day the following week. He greeted us with a broad smile when he arrived on the following day. As soon as we had settled down he announced, as if addressing a large audience, that he was going to "perform" the last act of Siegfried's Death and proceeded to do so. It was amazing how he could act each role, whether it was the hero Siegfried, the villain Hagen or the suffering heroine Brunnhilde. The last reading, describing the end of the world, and the beginning of a new one, was incredibly dramatic. We were all exhausted after the reading, he with effort and Otto and I with the emotional ride of the drama. I said that I needed a week to think it over before saying anything about the work and he promised to drop by next week.

I became obsessed with the poem. It was nothing like I had experienced before. It gave me a glimpse of a different world which was rising out of the ashes, but something was missing. What exactly was it? I spent sleepless nights wondering about it. One afternoon, while thinking about it, I fell asleep. In my sleep I saw the whole drama unfold before my eyes. I woke up with a start when I saw the castle on fire and was relieved to see that it was only a dream turning into a nightmare. I lay in bed, the whole drama playing before my eyes over and over again. Suddenly, I felt exultation. I knew what was missing. I did not know what motivated Siegfried and Brunnhilde and why the ring was so important to every one. I mentioned it to R. He readily agreed and said that another poem may be needed to set the stage and he would work on it right away.

Over the next three months R read to us the drama of Siegfried growing from an adolescent to a mature hero. Otto was really enthused about these sessions and adjusted his business schedule to be free for these mornings. We heard about Siegfried's discovery of the duplicity of his foster father Mime, forging of the sword, killing of the last giant, meeting with Brunnhilde, and the great duet. He kept insisting that it sounded rather plain in his readings but would be absolutely riveting with the music he had in mind. Occasionally, as with forging song and the duet, he accompanied himself on the piano. The suspense was unbearable and we literally lived from one reading to the next.


6


The evening of the first concert soon arrived. Otto and I got to the Concert Hall of the Zurich Music Society quite early and took our seats in the box. R had advised me that he wanted to spend his time before and during the performance with the artists and would see us after the performance. The hall started filling up and at the dot of seven o'clock the orchestra members stopped warming up and the concertmaster walked in, amidst great applause, with his violin. He tuned the orchestra and sat down. Just as the last waves of the tune up faded away, the small thin man with long black hair almost ran to the conductor's podium, raised his baton, and the glorious bang that opens Beethoven's Seventh Symphony filled the hall. The work starts slowly and then picks up tempo as if to let the dancers warm up before the fun starts. All ears were tuned to the sound and all eyes were riveted on the conductor. His motions were economical and precise. He smiled at players who did their part and seemed to frown at some whose touch slackened. This kept the huge orchestra of seventy five players on their toes and the audience captivated. This was a very popular work in Zurich and the audience knew it by heart. Yet, tempos were exaggerated but without being wild and the freshness in the performance gave me joy I had not felt before with other conductors. When the first movement came to an end, the audience was ready to erupt but he raised his hand, turned to face the audience and said in a clear authoritative voice, "Hold your applause to the end of the work please. Works of art deserve to be performed without interruption." Before the emotions could subside, he raised his baton and the second movement started at a slow steady pace as if to calm the excitement of the first movement. The third movement Scherzo set the stage for a dramatic allegro finale when all the pent up emotion of the orchestra came to the surface and took the audience with it as if in a relentless current. The hall erupted as the last note sounded. Everyone was standing up, cheering their hearts out. R took a bow and the orchestra members had to stand ten times before the audience calmed down enough to start moving towards the foyer for the intermission. Many were wondering whether the players had the emotional and physical energy left to do justice to Herr Wagner's own works.

As it turned out, the fears were unfounded. The orchestra returned in fine form to play the prelude to *Rienzi*, R's first success in Dresden. Weber's influence was clear but the composer's mastery of a large orchestra was there for all to admire. Next we were treated to the Bacchanal from *Tannhauser*. It dripped unabashed eroticism and the performance did nothing to hide it. Many ladies covered their faces to hide their feelings. But the applause showed that most people enjoyed it. Then came the wedding march from *Lohengrin*. The music was different than anything heard in Zurich before. Still, the charming melodies were orchestrated to bring out the best in them and every one in the audience wished for more. R heard this wish by the telepathic connection a great performer has with the audience. He performed the last two pieces again. Just as the conductor lowered his baton, every member of the audience jumped up and started cheering. Poor R had to come back to take the bows again and again till exhaustion overtook the audience and they staggered to the exit doors.

Otto must have been the most excited person in the audience. He felt immense pride in making it all possible. We made our way backstage to the conductor's room. The room was simply furnished with a change area, a piano and a few chairs. R was slumped in one of them surrounded by orchestra players, mostly younger lady players. He saw us as we entered the room and made the effort to get up but Otto and I insisted that he stayed as he was. Otto shook his hands with great vigour that told him how much he had enjoyed the concert. We insisted that he accompany us to our villa for milk and sauerkraut and pastries. He reluctantly said "Till next rehearsal" to his friends. Otto helped him put on his coat and hat. I noticed a new swagger in R's walk, no doubt born out of the confidence the evening's success had given him. On the way back he analyzed the performance in great detail. He concluded by expressing his satisfaction but expressed some anxiety about the choir in the next.

While R restricted himself to milk, Otto imbibed a fair amount of his favourite port. I am not sure to this day whether it was this port or Otto's secret ambition to patronize art that made him make an incredible offer to R. In addition to assistance in the rent, R would receive a monthly allowance as long as he continued to devote all his time to his art. In return, Otto would have rights to royalties from R's works but only until the allowance was repaid without any interest. R looked amazed at the generous offer and took a minute to recover. Then he gave a long speech on how nobles who patronized art were as important as the artists themselves because, without patrons, true artists would starve and art would shrivel, as would society. Otto thanked him for his sentiments and expressed the conviction that Herr Wagner's works would be as uplifting as the evening's performance.

7

R and I did not see each other till the next concert a week later. It was an even bigger success with the audience, if that is possible. The Prelude to *Lohengrin* was a novelty to most in the audience but the orchestra and conductor had the audience in their palms all the way. Then followed Erik's song from *Die Fliegende Hollander* with a tenor new to Zurich but well-known in Dresden who was visiting R. The incidental music from his operas *The Fairies, Forbidden Love* and *The Flying Dutchman* followed. He introduced each piece by describing the context in the opera in his lilting voice and the orchestra members followed his instructions to the note. It was a highly expectant crowd that retired for intermission. Excitement was palpable in the lobby and the gong inviting the audience to resume their seat was universally welcomed.

The stage was occupied by a full band of seventy five players and a huge choir of more than a hundred men and women. Men choristers were dressed in smart formal suits and the women were resplendent in emerald green dresses. As the audience settled down and the orchestra finished tuning, a big roar went up as the conductor and four soloists sauntered in. R waved to the choir to sit down, raised his baton, and my hands went to hold my heart in its place.

The great thing about Beethoven's work is the finale, a setting of Schiller's immortal words of joy to music, the first time a composer dared to demand an orchestra, choir and soloists in such a large number. In my previous experience of this work, both in Zurich and in Boston, I had felt confusion in several places and some crescendos seemed discordant as if different components of the orchestra were not appropriately balanced. This led to an overall impression that the mammoth task was perhaps just a little beyond the great Beethoven. Three movements that set the stage for the great finale can sound repetitious but I felt that a good conductor would be able to keep the audience intrigued. R's performance on the piano on the evening of Frau Marschall's dinner gave me hope that this evening the composer would be affirmed once and for all.

R fulfilled my hopes. On this lucky evening, two geniuses were working together and the orchestra members rose to the occasion in unison. R had smoothed out the wrinkles and balanced the orchestra. The performance uplifted my spirit like no other musical experience had ever done. It was as if I touched the spirit of the composer and I knew that from then on I would hear music with my soul rather than my ears. I had the sense that these feelings were going through every member of the audience. From the moment the bass opened his voice in exhortation to the last notes from the choir, the audience was as if it had been raised to the ceiling. As the last notes died down, the hall erupted in tremendous applause. Leaving the cheering crowd, we made our way back stage to the conductor's room where a strange sight met us. Some of the performers were standing around in a little circle and R was doing a headstand on the back of a chair. He jumped off the chair, did some somersaults, straightened himself and said, "Oh, I do wish there was a tree I could climb up. There is nothing I want to do after a good concert more than climb up a tall tree and scream like an ape."

"Herr Wagner, you can scream like a thousand apes, you will still not be heard above the audience still cheering for you."

"Herr Wesendonck, so pleased to see you. You are right. I must go and acknowledge them." He put on his coat and rushed off to the stage. We heard him thanking the audience profusely for their appreciation of his art, complimenting orchestra members for their hard work and thanking Otto and me for our friendship and support during his stay in Zurich. The applause gradually died down and R joined us still exhilarated by the success of the concerts.

8

The reaction of his associates to two concerts made Otto even more determined to support R in his endeavour to change the opera world of Germany. The performances of Beethoven's great works convinced Otto that R was a musical genius and the response of the audience to R's own compositions demonstrated that his new works deserved the support Otto had promised. R, on the other hand, took the praise as his due and talked of writing essays on conducting and on how to perform Beethoven's Ninth. He felt that most conductors were too timid to correct the mistakes Beethoven had made in balancing components of the orchestra because of his deafness. I suggested to him that it might not go well with these conductors and they might retaliate by not supporting his works. R pulled a face and said that his art was above these petty considerations.

On Otto's suggestion, I invited R and Minna for dinner. They arrived at the appointed hour. R was immaculately dressed in a silk shirt and evening suit. Minna was dressed in an ill-fitting evening dress obviously made by an amateur dress maker, if not by herself. As the evening wore on, it became clear that Minna was the direct opposite of R. She was completely absorbed in her own little problems, had nothing to say about anything of importance and nothing positive to say of R's ambitions as an artist. She could not hide her contempt in her reaction to his answers to our queries about his progress and his plans. However, her complete mastery over housekeeping on a tight budget became evident. She had every detail of the household on her fingertips. R truly depended on her to look after the home. In return, she expected him to provide the means, but to no avail. Otto and I saw the glaring mismatch and, I am sorry to say, our sympathies were with R and not with this woman who had suffered much by her husband's single-minded pursuit of his artistic goals and whose suffering during twenty years of marriage had reduced an actress of some reputation to no more than an excellent maid.

## 9

Our weekly morning sessions resumed. Otto was now very busy expanding his business in Italy and Spain and rarely joined us. Again, we too turns reading our creations. R read *Die Walkure*, the first of his trilogy, and then *Rheingold*, a two hour introduction to the trilogy as the operas eventually became. I read poems of my school days which I revised before reading to him. He suggested places that needed reconsideration and I mostly admired what I heard. These sessions lasted a couple of hours and before long attracted Otto's notice. One day at lunch, Otto remarked, "Matty, is Herr Wagner imposing too much on you?"

"Do you mind it dear? I find him amusing and he is so helpful with my writings." I replied.

"Herr Wagner has a lot to do. Please make sure not to take too much of his time, won't you, dear?"

"No risk of that darling Otto. Men, even geniuses, need a woman to boost their ego. Poor Herr Wagner has an ignoramus of a wife and I am the only woman around who cares to understand his work, howsoever vaguely. I feel it is my responsibility to fill this need if this genius is to achieve his potential."

"If you are happy with it, it is fine with me. We want to help him achieve the greatness that is his due. Some of his immortality might rub on us as well. No one will remember us a hundred years from now except for our support of Herr Wagner."

"Oh, Otto, you are so understanding. I love you so dearly, darling. I promise I will love you for ever, sweetheart. I will spoil you to bits, only if you will let me."

"You are so kind, dear Matty, to love this undeserving man. But we do have something going for us. I promise to do my bit to promote your, our, happiness."

We both simultaneously got up and embraced each other and exchanged a long sweet kiss till a muffled cough of the maid bringing coffee brought us back to earth. I insisted on him visiting my bedroom for a nap and we made up for this cruel interruption.


10


The autumn that year passed quietly for us but the winter was bitterly cold with heavy snow. It was so cold that Otto did not ski even once. Myrrha had not been feeling well and we skipped most Christmas and New Year parties. It was nearing the end of the month when R arrived with a huge folder of music. Otto was away on business and I greeted him warmly because it was his first visit of the New Year. The folder contained the score of *Rheingold,* the introductory one act opera that would last more than two hours without a break. I asked him how he expected the audience, particularly ladies, to sit so long. He replied, "That is not going to be a problem. They will be mesmerized and will be sorry it was so short when it ends." Then he went to the piano and started playing. Magical opening notes captivated me straight away. He sang in his inimitable way the role of each Rheinmaiden, then the dwarf Alberich, his grab for the gold and the Rheinmaiden's shrieks. It did mesmerize me and held me in my chair fully focused on the music. He stopped at the shrieks and sat for a while looking at me for the reaction. When none was forthcoming, he said that was enough introduction to the music of the future for one day. We would do Scene Two in a week. I got up, went to him still sitting at the piano, looked in his eyes, and said, "I have seen the future and it is heavenly." He got up, took my hands gently in his and replied, "There is a lot of tough walking before we get there. I need the support of an angel to give me wings to clear the way. Will you be that angel?" Tears welled into my eyes; I looked the other way and ran out to my room. I did not hear him leave.

R was busy scoring the music when his eczema was not playing up. Minna's heart palpitations became worse and she went on a cure to Lake Lucerne. These problems made her temperamental and her relationship with R became even more hostile. It was three months when he showed up again but only to listen to my poetry. He was too distraught to play the next scene but he was making good progress with scoring at last. It took us several visits for each scene and it was the end of the year when we finished *Rheingold*. We had been very circumspect of each other after the first scene but the last scene, when the gods climb the rainbow bridge to Valhalla broke the reticence in both of us. As he finished the oration of Wotan and the cries of the Rheinmaidens, he stood up. I took both his hands in mine and looked into his eyes and whispered, "I will be your angel."

11

R's next visit was on a beautiful winter morning. Ice crystals hung from the trees like diamonds reflecting rays from a brilliant sun. The sky was shimmering blue with not a cloud in sight. We bundled up and set for a walk on the carpet of snow. Before long we were holding hands like adolescents in the first blush of love. He excitedly told me that he had been reading a philosopher who seemed to unite his own rather disconnected thoughts. He then told me in an offhand manner that the English wanted him to go to London to conduct for six months for a generous fee of two hundred pounds but he was not going to accept because he could not live away from me. I was dumbstruck. We walked silently for a while which gave me time to think. It occurred to me that, in addition to the badly needed funds, it would be good for him to go because London was becoming a new hub of musical activity and it would be a new experience for him. It might even broaden his circle of patrons.

He listened impatiently to me but wavered when I promised to write him frequently if he would accept the invitation. We agreed that, through thoughtful correspondence, we might come to understand each other's inner souls. He flattered me by saying that I had persuaded him to go and he would do his all to make progress in the music of Die Walkure and make new friends. When we returned, I showed him a gold pen I had bought at a jeweler in New York and asked, "Will you use it to write to me from London?"

He was thrilled, "Oh it is so beautiful. It will always be something very special. It will be used only for letters to you. And the music dramas that will restore the glory of German art will come out of this pen. There is nothing material that I can give you, except the first complete work from this pen."

R showed up unexpectedly on the morning of Chrismas eve. He saw that it was not an opportune time to visit and apologized profusely. Then he produced a folder and with a great show of humility presented it to me. "A symphony I had written in my young days. I revised it to make it presentable. Do me the honour of accepting this humble offering," he said. Before I could find a word to say, he turned around and was gone.

On our last meeting before his departure to London, he had a new folder with him. It contained the sketch of his next opera. The story was based on the legend of King Marke's favourite courtier Tristan and the Irish princess Isolde. R rewrote the tale for his opera in three acts. Tristan is bringing the Princess to Cornwall to marry the king. However, they fall in love during the journey. Isolde marries the king after they land, but she still loves Tristan. They are caught in a tryst and Tristan is seriously wounded in the subsequent duel with another courtier. Tristan is carried to his island where he is longing for Isolde. She comes, but a little late and dies of grief when she sees Tristan breathing his last. The lovers are united for ever in death.

I knew R was thinking of us in the sketch. What I did not know was how closely our lives were to follow his art.

## 12

The letters became longer as the days went by. They were mostly about progress with the music of *Die Walkure*, lazy and poorly trained orchestra players, uncouth journalists, beautiful parks, and welcoming natives. He was so very discreet about our relation that, if Otto read any of the letters, he would have found no reason for jealousy. I had not told Otto about becoming R's muse because I was trying to think of the best way to do it and there was no rush as long as we were discreet and the North Sea was between us. He often wrote of meetings with a fellow composer from Paris and long interesting discussions with him. The poor monsieur, having to sit still for hours when R propounded his convictions. R had no patience with other opinions, whether they were in agreement or opposed to his own. But he needed listeners for his detailed pronouncements. That is how he worked out his thought processes, talking in long sentences to a passive listener. That is why he changed his views so often.

The last letter was thick enough to be a small book. He was thrilled to meet Queen Victoria, her consort and attending nobility for his last concert and his pleasure was unbounded when the Queen told him how much better the orchestra sounded under him than with Felix. "Dear Felix, such a great composer, but such a lazy conductor," he quoted the Queen gleefully. "Lazy composer too, Your Majesty," he wrote was his reply.

But I didn't think even R would be so tactless as to say that.

Now that R was on his way back to Zurich I had to tell Otto of my promise to R. I loved Otto, my two children and the comfort Otto was, emotionally and materially. Over coffee after lunch, when the nurse had taken the children to nursery, I said to my cup, "Otto dear, you know Herr Wagner is returning from London today."

"Oh! I hope he enjoyed his visit. London is a great city. I should take you there soon," Otto replied.

"Otto, something you should know and I need to tell you now. Please don't read too much into it and don't get upset with him or me."

"Of course not, dear. You have never given me any reason to be upset. We are not going to start now, are we?"

"Otto, I am so glad you think so. You know Herr Wagner's married life is very unhappy. His wife is not a real partner."

"I guessed that much, dear."

"He can't discuss his work, or his thoughts and feelings with her. Poor man. If he is to give his all to his art he needs some one to share his inner self with."

"And you are proposing to be that one!"

"Otto, do you mind, dear. I will so love to see a man of his genius create what he is capable of."

"I have an uncomfortable feeling, dear. It could cause a scandal. But I know you and trust you. I will be proud to have a wife who is the muse to the creator of immortal works of art. Only two requests, though."

"Yes dear."

"No scandals."

"Of course not, dear."

"And no sharing of beds."

"How can you even think that, Otto dear? Herr Wagner is as old as dear Papa."

"Sorry dear. I was being honest about my feelings as you are about yours."

"Thank you Otto, you must be the most understanding man on earth. I love you more than you will ever know."

"I often wonder why. No one else will even look at this ugly old sod."

"Even uglier and older than Herr Wagner!"

We both burst out laughing. Shortly afterwards, we sealed our agreement in bed.

## 13

R did not show up for a week after his return. He said that he was having trouble with Minna again. She was upset that he didn't write to her when he was away and her heart murmurs were getting worse. She complained of his spendthrift ways which ate away the anticipated profits of the venture and now she couldn't afford to leave for her cure. He himself seemed to be in better health. English food suited his digestion and his eczema had also improved. I did not mention it to him but it indicated a really rocky relationship when the separation improved his health and worsened that of his wife. He felt the trouble of the visit was worthwhile because it exposed English audiences to his music. I breathed a sigh of relief when he said that he had put the *Tristan and Isolde* sketch aside for now and was focusing on completing his trilogy. He was happy about the progress with the music and played the Prelude. I was struck with the opening, so full of foreboding, and the following storm. He stopped when Siegmunde came on stage. He banged the piano shut, stamped his feet to express his frustration. He said he was frustrated because he couldn't play piano well and was not doing justice to his music. Before I could say a consoling word, the clouds scattered, he smiled and said, "May not be as good as Liszt, but still better than Berlioz." I later learnt that Monsieur Berlioz did not play piano at all.

The next few months were uneventful. Winter came and went. The greatest joy we had was to see Myrrha and Guido skiing with their Papa. R came over two or three times a month to show what he had written and to listen to whatever progress I had made in the play I was writing. I did not get much time to write because of my preoccupation with R's creation. I had an uneasy feeling about Siegmunde. I felt that his character was not fully developed; his love for Sieglinde needed some sacrifice from him. I suggested a dialogue with Wotan or Wotan's daughter Brunnhilde where he turns down eternal life in Valhalla without Sieglinde. R was delighted with the suggestion and I was flattered when he showed me how he had incorporated it in the second act. He celebrated the arrival of late spring by completing the score of *Die Walkure*. He played the third and final act to Otto and me one cold afternoon when a thick mist covered the lake. The opera ends with Wotan's lament as he puts Brunnhilde to sleep surrounded by a ring of fire. At the end of the moving scene, Otto and I sat still staring at the piano and R looking at the window overlooking the lake from the piano bench. After a long period of teary silence, R turned to us and said, "Wotan is me, Wotan is every one of us." All of a sudden he smiled through tears, wiped his face with his elegant silk handkerchief and said, "Wonder how much worse I would have felt if I had any children of my own." He got up, bowed deeply to both of us and left as the sun peeped through the clouds above the lake.

## 14

R did not call on us for several weeks. When he did arrive, he looked haggard and in need of food and sleep. He told us that the neighbours in his apartment building were very noisy themselves but never failed to complain about his piano when he was composing. On top of it, the blacksmith across the street hammered away just when R needed peace and quiet. This added to his stress and he was taking it out on his poor wife. This led to continuous fighting between the two and he had not been sleeping well. His work had come to a halt and his eczema had flared up again. After feeding him sauerkraut and hot milk, I asked if he would like to move into an old cottage on the grounds where we were building our new home. His face brightened up. After a few questions about the space he asked when he could move. I promised to discuss it with Otto and find out when it could be made ready for them. When he left, it looked as if he was walking on air. I was able to send him a message the next day that they could move there in May, two weeks away, and Otto would charge the same rent as he was paying now on the condition that he made satisfactory progress with his writing.

## 15

Our family moved into Green Hill, our new home, and R's family moved to the cottage he called Refuge. The cottage was small but he and Minna found it ample for their needs. It was built on a slope such that the upper floor had its own entrance facing Green Hill. There was a large room that R used as his studio and moved in it his favourite desk and chair and an old and somewhat dilapidated piano which must have been difficult to keep in tune. I promised myself that I would get Otto to replace it with a new Erard Grand on R's next birthday. The other room on the floor was smaller and they furnished it as a guest room. The cottage had enough living and sleeping room on the main floor below. It fronted a wide lawn on the other side of Green Hill. Minna liked her privacy and had the windows covered by thick curtains. My music room faced the cottage. It was here that I also did my correspondence and other writing. I could see R working in his studio from my desk and hear the piano when he was trying to iron out a melody. I loved it the way he played with the notes till everything was perfect. I often wondered whether he noticed that after hours of tinkering, he usually returned to what he had started with.

His visits now became a daily affair. He often stayed for meals. He was an easy guest because he didn't mind what was served as long as we provided an attentive audience. He played with Myrrha and Guido and they loved it. It was easy for me to skip to his studio without disturbing Minna. I noticed that I was visiting him to read my creations almost as often as he was visiting us. I needed his encouragement to work on *Gudrun*, my play which later enjoyed some success on stage. Heaven knows I could not have finished it without him.

After completing the first two acts of *Siegfried*, R put his composing aside for a while. He approached a number of opera houses with proposals of week long festivals to perform his trilogy with Prelude over four evenings of performances followed by three evenings of discussions. He was very discouraged with the response. The opera houses were happy to present *Lohengrin* frequently, and his other operas sometimes, but they were not convinced that a festival on the grand scale of his operas was a commercial proposition. So it was not altogether a shock when, on a stroll along the banks of the lake one summer evening, I heard him announce in a matter of fact manner, "I have put aside my life's work for now. I am working on the poem of *Tristan and Isolde*. I will finish it in a few weeks. It is a simple opera and every opera house will want to stage it. The money it will bring will relieve Minna of her anxieties and may even cure her heart murmurs." I knew it was fruitless to persuade him to go back to complete *Siegfried*. All I could get from him was the promise that he would return to it as soon as *Tristan* was finished.

R worked like a maniac. He wanted to finalize the sketch in a couple of weeks, finish the poem in four more and then work on the music. This year was the most exhilarating and most difficult year of my life. Both our worlds were turned upside down but I kept my promise to Otto and it righted my life, at least on the surface.

## 16

During the time R was writing the poem, we saw each other several times a day. It was all about his poem. He would sit forever holding my hand without saying a word and looking into my eyes. I do not know what he was looking for but I was amazed at how much understanding there was in his deep blue eyes set in a large head with unruly hair. I could see the love for me in those eyes and behind them a need to understand humanity. Then suddenly he would drop my hands and say, "You are showing me the way." He would take out the gold pen and start scribbling on paper. Sometimes he insisted I stayed. Other times he was totally oblivious to everything, and I left unnoticed. On our walks, he would insist we walked quietly holding hands for a long time. In this period of silence I felt as if he was raking my brain to look for thoughts covered by leaves. Rather than distract him by asking what was it that he was looking for, I let him work it out. Once in a while he would scream, "Yes, this is what Isolde would say." Other times he would stamp his foot and whisper, "Isolde is somewhere else today." On these occasions, he apologized for his rudeness, bending, almost falling on his knees.

Cosima, daughter of R's friend Franz Liszt and her new hus-band, the pianist Hans van Bulow, were visiting R in September. R had taken the young pianist under his wings and was training him in the art of conducting as well as promoting his career as a pianist. R invited Otto and me to listen to his new poem along with his visitors and Minna. We sat around him when he read his poem about doomed lovers – acting each role to perfection. He avoided Minna but looked meaningfully at me throughout the love duet in the second act. Otto's discomfort was obvious when R looked at him during King Marke's recitation at the end. Both Cosima and Hans were entranced by the poem and burst out in applause at the end. Otto and I joined them in congratulating R heartily. Minna was obviously angry and left without a word. On our walk back to the villa, Otto said quietly, "I hope life does not follow Herr Wagner's art too closely for our comfort."

R immediately started to set to music "our poem," as he called it, when we were together. It seemed that the music was already in his head. It flowed from the gold pen as fast as the ink. Now we were spending most of the day together, either in our music room or in his study. This upset the family routine at Green Hill. We had meals when R was hungry. He even started telling servants what we would have. The room was either too hot or too cold and the fire had to be arranged to suit him irrespective of how Otto felt. Otto put up with these inconveniences, perhaps because he had the gut feeling that a unique work of art was being created. R played what he considered the key moments and Otto was intrigued by the music. It was very different than any music we had ever heard. As the composition progressed, we wondered whether it was humanly possible to sing the roles as he had written them, whether the music could be played by any orchestra. Whenever we voiced these concerns he would say, "I have to write what I hear in my inner ear. I will tackle the problems of performance when the time comes."

## 17

He finished the music by the end of the year and started orchestration straight away. Something remarkable happened during the four months R took to complete the first act. When the curtain rises, Isolde is angry with her former lover Tristan for his treachery in taking her from Ireland to Cornwall to marry King Marke. When R started work on the opera, it was as if he wound up in my head; at such moments my feelings were those of an admirer for a genius. We held hands when acting out our roles in our walks to facilitate his creativity, but were duly circumspect at other times.

As the work on this act progressed, he moved ever so slowly from my head to my heart just as love replaced Isolde's anger. R held me in his arms and looked into my eyes longingly with increasing frequency. My protestations, very firm at first, became milder and eventually ceased. Before long, I was putting down on paper what was buzzing in my head. It was as if my head and my heart had been taken over by some force out there and I could do nothing on my own. One day I was woken up by the glorious music of the birds outside the window. I looked out and was overwhelmed by the beauty of the blooming flowers and the pink glow of the dawn. I dressed quickly and rushed to the lake.

Watching the sun rise over the lake this beautiful morning, I felt as I hadn't felt since I was sixteen. Words poured out of my head and I whispered them to the spirit of my lover. I returned to the room when the sun became bright and put the words on paper. Reading the words I wondered if R had transmitted to his Isolde the sentiments of Tristan's Isolde in her farewell to this world before joining her Tristan in the next life:

> And each flower's tender blossom,
> While exhaling fragrant breath,
> Like a twilight in thy bosom,
> Fades to silent rapturous death.

This poem of five such stanzas became *Dreams*, the last in my collection of five poems. I wrote them down in calligraphy on sheets of beautiful pink paper as if under a spell. When the ink had dried, I read them again. And I felt overtaken by a sense of shame. Here I was, in the shadow of an immortal poet and composer, writing like a teenager. What would he think if he saw this childish verse? I collected the papers and put them in the bottom drawer.

R finished the score of first act the day before Easter. We both cried when R read of the boat approaching the port in the final scene. With tears running down my cheeks, I went to my room and brought my poems and pushed them in his hands, "These are for you. You must know what these are. You dictated them to me."

He was startled. "I did not dictate anything to anybody, not even you." Then he looked at the poems. "These are wonderful. Only a young woman in the first blush of love could pen them." Then he added, "These need to be set to music. This is my next project. Your poetry and my music will combine into great art."

He became very secretive for the next couple of weeks and did not discuss or play his composition. He stopped playing in the middle of a melody if he heard my footsteps and I could not make out much from the music floating to Green Hill from his cottage. One fine morning, he greeted me cheerfully when I opened the door of his study and presented me with a sheaf of music score with a deep bow, "Humble token of deep love of a simple artist for the woman of his dreams." I looked at the front page and my body went numb when I saw the title. The score for my poems fell from my hands and scattered all over the floor. Neither of us moved to collect them. I looked at him with a smile through the tears in my eyes. He broke the silence, "I hope the music is a credit to the poems, it comes straight from my heart just as the words came from yours." He then played the music and sang the poems from memory. I had recovered enough of my composure to join him for *Dreams*, the last song. After "silent rapturous death," he got up from the bench, put his arms around me and moved to kiss me. Tears welled out again as I turned my face and said, "No, no, R. There are some things not permitted to lovers, these lovers." I picked up the music and went straight to my room.

## 18

R now started work on Act Two. In this act, the two lovers arrange a tryst and declare their love for each other. The King's party returns and Tristan is challenged to a duel and is mortally wounded. R said he was having difficulty with this Act and would need much inspiration from me as well as from divine powers. I soon found out what he meant.

R was always very respectful and discreet in the presence of third parties. But when we were alone, he would address me in Tristan's words to Isolde with all the feelings he had poured into them when writing the poem. Something moved me to return Isolde's response. After a few minutes of this duet, he would hum it if he were outdoors or play on the piano if we were at either home. The poem was creating feelings in us and these feelings shaped the music which he put down on paper. The feelings were so strong that on many occasions I wished he would hold me tightly in his arms and let love take its own course. I am sure he could see it, just as I could see feelings race through his body. But something, perhaps my reaction to his advance when he played the music for *Dream*, stopped us. We remained chaste in body and suppressed the needs of our soul.

It was towards the end of July when he was nearly at the end of the Second Act. Minna was away the evening he played it to me. The pressure in us built up with the love scene and by the time Tristan was wounded I was beside myself. I held him tight in my arms sobbing loudly, "Tristan, Tristan, I will come with you." He was sobbing too, "True lovers only unite in death; life is a test we have to go through." We heard the front door open and steps on the stairs. We separated quickly and greeted Minna as calmly as was possible under the circumstances.

19

I had difficulty going to sleep. The music was so haunting it would not let me rest in peace. Suddenly, the music stopped. I was floating in air. Not on a cushion, not on wings either, just floating in air unadorned by any clothing. Then I heard R calling, "Mathilde my love, at last we are united." R embraced me and we were united in love. I felt the thrill of making love course through my body again and again. Then there was peace, peace disturbed by Otto's anxious voice, "Are you all right, darling? I have never seen you sleep so late."

Back to drudgery of living again. Yes, life without R on my side every moment had become drudgery.

Later the same day Otto and I had just sat down to lunch when Minna burst in. She was extremely agitated. She addressed herself to Otto, "Sir, you have been very kind and generous to my husband and we are grateful to you. Will you spare me some more of your generosity and bestow on this poor suffering woman one last favour. All I ask for is a minute of your time if you will grant me the privilege. Can we go somewhere private?" I left the room to them. As I was closing the door I heard her burst into loud sobs.

Otto saw me after she had left. Minna had given Otto a letter from R addressed to me which got into her hands through the carelessness of their maid. The letter was a very frank description of our love-making the previous night. I was bewildered. R had the same dream as I did. Only he thought it fit to put it down in the most florid language and send it to me. Otto was sure that the letter was an artist's imagination gone berserk, after all I was in the room next to his all night. But he did say something had to be done. He had already heard gossip about R and me and had disregarded it. Now it was sure to get out of hand. I agreed with Otto that something had to be done to shut the vile mouths. Otto decided to think it over for a day or two. No sooner had we settled on this, we heard screaming and sounds of dishes being thrown about in Refuge, the cottage.

Otto came to my room the next morning when I was dressing for breakfast. My heart sank when I looked at his face and the dreaded words went through my ears and echoed in my brain, "Herr Wagner has to go."

"Only till things settle down! He can move back in his old apartment."

"No, he has to leave Zurich. It will be a while before the wagging tongues stop."

"He always said he wanted to spend his life in that cottage. How will he manage? He doesn't have any money."

"I will help him, for your sake. But he will have to keep away and not bother you in any way."

"But Otto dear, he hasn't finished the opera he is working on. He needs some one to talk about it."

"Separation will help him in composing the music for separated lovers, don't you think?"

"Otto, you are so cruel."

"Sometimes cruelty is what an artist needs. Why else would he ask for it?"

"Otto, I gave you my word that there would be no gossip. I can't deny that there is. You have me trapped. I will go along with whatever you say. But be kind and look after their needs, please Otto."

Otto sensibly left me alone to cry my heart out and to come to terms with events. He had gone when I entered the breakfast room.

R came to me a couple of days later. He had tears in his eyes.

He had come to say farewell. He was going to Venice to complete Tristan's orchestration. He didn't know how long it would be. Minna was moving to Dresden. I didn't tell him I knew all this and that the ten thousand francs Otto gave him was on my insistence. He promised to write to me every day to keep our love alive. I promised to do likewise. I didn't have the heart to tell him of Otto's ban on our correspondence.

20

There was no communication with R for several weeks. Then our former neighbour Madame Wille dropped by on her way to see her son. After making sure no one was listening, she told me that R was heartbroken because all his letters to me had been returned unopened. It came to me as no surprise and I told her of my deal with Otto. Madame Wille agreed that this was the only thing to do if gossip going around Zurich high society was to be stopped. However, if I wished to stay in touch with R, she offered her services. I agreed, perhaps with unseemly haste. Then she produced a bundle of letters for me. I promised that she would have regular mail from now on to forward to Venice.

I went to my room, arranged the letters carefully by date and read them. R swore eternal love, said he couldn't imagine life away from me and wished that Otto did not insist on him living abroad. I wrote to him encouraging letters swearing the love of Isolde for her Tristan and trusting our eventual union. I found that this separation created distance between Otto and me too. He started traveling more frequently and was drinking more than was good for him. But I could not gather the courage to leave Otto, Myrrha and Guido. I consoled myself that I had to do what I could to see the genius create great art but I had to safeguard my family too, even if it meant sacrificing my one true love.

A few months went by. R and I exchanged almost daily letters promising ourselves to the other and keeping informed of the other's artistic endeavours. R was making progress with the score of the third act and I was writing fairy tales for Myrrha. But then whatever peace poor R had was shattered. The authorities in Venice were being pressured to arrest him and return him to Dresden. He had to move again in a hurry. On my advice, he asked Otto if he could stay with us for a short while but Otto refused even to let him come to Zurich.

His next letter was from Lucerne. He had escaped from Venice just ahead of the police sent to arrest him. The letter was as flowery as ever, professing his undying love for his Isolde. He was now setting his love-death poem and he hoped that this would be his masterpiece to compare to the music of *Dream* which was only to be shared by the two of us and which the world would never see.

It was a year since he had left Refuge. I had not seen him for a year and my arms were aching to hold him again. I begged Otto to let me join him on a visit to Lucerne and arrange to meet R. Otto agreed reluctantly, partly because a meeting in a place 50 kilometers away would not be noticed by the wagging tongues of Zurich and partly hoping that it might revive my sagging spirits. Once we were in Lucerne he sent R a note inviting him to visit us.

Being a thoroughly decent man, Otto left me alone to meet R on the appointed morning. R entered the room, closed the door behind him and rushed to crush me in his arms. I returned the favour. "Oh, it has been so long," we both sighed. We sat looking at each other, no words needed to be said. He looked starved, as he did the first time I saw him at Herr Marschall's dinner. At last I asked him why he kept it from me that he had been sick. "I did not want Isolde to worry, she had enough on her plate already," he said. He then told me that he had completed the opera and he was quite satisfied with his setting of love-death. I promised him that I would attend the premiere wherever it was. He swore on his word of honour that Tristan would not be premiered without Isolde in the audience, even if she was escorted by King Marke. He told me his plans. He was going to Paris to conduct some concerts and get his opera *Tannhauser* performed. He felt certain that the Royal Opera in Vienna would put "our drama" on stage. He had no plans to settle down anywhere, if he couldn't live near me.

His almost daily letters from Paris gave me the progress report on his concerts and the preparations for the opera. Minna joined him there and he was physically comfortable but his heart was with me in Zurich. I heard of all the problems in the translation of *Tannhauser*, his disappointment at having someone else conduct the performance, the need to insert a ballet to keep up with tradition, the poor quality of the rehearsals and then botched performances. He was so disappointed that he withdrew the opera even though every performance was sold out and it could have solved his financial difficulties. Minna was very upset with him and went back to Dresden. One item of good news was the partial pardon he had received; he could now return to Germany although not to Saxony.

## 21

R spent the next three years moving from one place to the other. He finally separated from Minna and set a comfortable allowance for her out of his income from the royalties from *Lohengrin* which was becoming very popular. He had a successful conducting tour of Russia. His letters became less frequent but there was no reduction in ardour. He was still looking forward to the union in the next life but I started noticing a note of cynicism. My letters to him were warm as ever. However, his preoccupations elsewhere became more urgent as time went on. Then, at last, fortune smiled at him. King Ludwig of Bavaria took him under his wings, paid off his debts and granted him a large allowance. He fell in love, or so he pretended, with Cosima, the daughter of his friend and the wife of his disciple. I remembered their presence at R's reading of "our opera" and was amused at the thought of R reading the love story to his past, present and future loves and their husbands.

Cosima insisted that he terminate correspondence with me. I responded that my love for him was still as pure and fresh as when he played and I sang *Dream*. His response, the last letter from him, was rude and crude, no doubt dictated by his new love. I later learnt that this awful woman was bent on changing R's past to fit her image. Not only did she smooth the wrinkles from R's life, she removed any evidence of these. My letters to R were particular thorns in her side and she burnt every one of them.

I loved R in spite of all this crudity. If truth were to be told, I felt sorry for him that the new woman in his life was not a fraction as reasonable as my Otto. Although he reneged on his promise to invite me, Otto and I went to Munich for the premiere of *Tristan and Isolde* and *Die Meistersinger* which were great successes, and the first two *Ring* operas which were miserable failures. R was very distant when we went backstage to congratulate him. This prompted Otto's remark, "Herr Wagner has got over his infatuation at last." I nodded, but not with any joy.

Sixteen years after R's departure from Zurich, we went to his new theatre in Beyreuth for the first performance of the complete *Ring*, the new name for the Prelude and the Trilogy he was writing in Zurich. This time he was very effusive in our meetings and thanked Otto and me in the presence of his wife and father-in-law for our support at a critical time in his life. I am sorry to this day that I did not have an opportunity to tell him that he still occupied a large space in my heart. I do believe that he reciprocated these feelings in his heart, irrespective of the face he put forward to his wife and the world.

## 22

I heard of his death after a heart attack on an unlucky date of an unlucky month of the miserable year 1883. It was reported in all the newspapers that his wife had a furious argument with him that morning. I can never forgive her for being so selfish as to quarrel with an old man with known heart problems. Imagine her putting out the story that he died in her arms! Even if he did, I know he was thinking of his Isolde and she was his last memory to take to the next world. *Dream* lives with me as it lived with my Tristan to his last day.

*Please forgive me the note of bitterness towards his widow. I had given my whole heart to Richard, even though I could not bring myself to give up my children for him. I loved him even when I was reading letters from Madame Wille of his romantic escapades. I cried more at his death than when Otto took his leave. But I had to keep his love hidden in my heart, till now at any rate. Now I want the world to know that Richard had his Isolde, and Mathilde had her Tristan, if only in a Dream. The world will see the letters Isolde has so carefully preserved over the last forty years and the world will hear the music he set for our Dream and our love will resonate till the end of time.*

**Isolde's Dream and Other Stories** is Sudhir Jain's first collection of stories. The title story is the love affair between composer Richard Wagner and Mathilde, young wife of his patron Otto Wesendonck and is narrated by Mathilde. The other love story in the collection is the tragic affair between young Gustav Mahler, another composer, and Marion von Weber seen through her eyes. The other stories are humorous, based on life experiences of people the author has come across but generally told in first person with a rare sense of self-deprecating wit.

Comments on the book:
*Isolde's Dream* is Sudhir Jain's account of his life experiences. Through story, anecdote and philosophical reflection, he describes his journey from India to Canada and also his inward journey as he reflects on his family, his love of music and many other topics. It is a compelling narrative of personal growth and interior exploration.
**Anne Stott**, University of London, Author of *Hannah More, the First Victorian*.

Sudhir Jain has written a unique and delicious sandwich for readers. In *Isolde's Dream* two intriguing operatic pieces surround a humorous mix of insightful contemporary stories. Bon appetit!
**Barb Howard**, Creative Writing teacher and author of *Whipstock*, a tall tale set in Alberta's oil patch.

Comment about the author:
You are a beautiful writer.
**Linda Goyette**, editor and columnist.

About the author:
**Sudhir Jain** is a retired Geophysicist whose passion for literature and music goes back to early childhood. Thanks to his extensive literary interests, he switched easily from publishing award-winning technical papers to writing letters to the editors on many topics with his unique but widely appreciated points of view. His stories, based on the observations during his life in five countries, are notable for a combination of wit, humour and pathos. He and his wife have made their home in Calgary for over thirty years. They have three daughters and two granddaughters. He has appeared on radio and TV a number of times.

ISBN 978-1-896209-91-3

BAYEUX